GARDEN PRINCESS

GARDEN PRINCESS

Kristin Kladstrup

CANDLEWICK PRESS

Copyright © 2013 by Kristin Kladstrup

First paperback edition 2015

Library of Congress Catalog Card Number 2012943642
ISBN 978-0-7636-5685-0 (hardcover)
ISBN 978-0-7636-7668-1 (paperback)

14 15 16 17 18 19 BVG 10 9 8 7 6 5 4 3 2 1

Printed in Berryville, VA, U.S.A.

This book was typeset in Hightower.

Candlewick Press
99 Dover Street
Somerville, Massachusetts 02144

visit us at www.candlewick.com

For Kathy, Su, Sarah, and Frankie

Many Years Before

He had never seen so much wealth in one place.

There was so much jewelry here that he could take as much as he wanted and no one would ever notice anything was missing. He picked up a golden bracelet, a necklace with a pearl the size of a bird's egg, and a silver brooch shaped like a star. He slipped them all into his pocket, then glanced over his shoulder at the open window across the room. He was sure nobody had seen him leave the garden party. It had been easy enough to slip away, but he had yet to meet his hostess. What if she noticed he was missing and sent a servant to find him? He had better hurry.

But as he turned back to the table piled with jewels, he caught sight of his reflection in the mirror above it. He stared. Was that what he looked like? There was no mirror at home; he had seen his own face only a few times before in his life. And he had never seen himself like this, looking like a splendid gentleman in these fine clothes. . . .

Stolen clothes! He had lied to his mother when she had, guessed they were stolen, pretending he had bought them with money made from work he had never done. But it would be the last time he lied to her, he told himself now. This would be the last time he stole anything. After today, they would have enough. He could pay a doctor, and his mother would get well, and they would have enough to eat, and they would never have to worry again.

He picked up a diamond ring, watching it sparkle in the light from the window. "The last time," he whispered.

And then the door behind him was thrown open. Startled, he looked up and saw a woman in the mirror. He had no doubt it was the woman who had invited him here. Someone had told him she was a great beauty, and he supposed that she was. But now, as their eyes met in the glass, he was too frightened to turn and look at her directly.

"You're a thief," she said.

He shook his head and put down the ring. "No, I—"

Her laugh sent a chill through him. "A thief and a liar."

He watched in the mirror as she raised her hand. Then his eyes locked on his own terrified expression.

"Steal from me, and you'll be a thief forever."

chapter 1

THE INVITATION

Princess Adela laced her fingers under a clump of creeping Charlie and pulled, enjoying the satisfying crackle of roots ripping free of soil. She tossed the weed onto a heap of similarly vanquished garden invaders and pulled out another clump.

She had been up since dawn weeding this particular flower bed, only one of the many beds the palace gardener had given over to her care and planning. She was getting this one ready for the bulbs she wanted to plant — red tulips, yellow daffodils, and grape hyacinths. The tulips would not be the tall, stately ones that graced the more formal beds of the palace gardens but a shorter variety with curving petals and patterned leaves. In spring, the tulips, daffodils, and hyacinths would give the illusion of having come up by chance, like wildflowers. Adela loved having a wild look to her garden.

She also loved mornings. Even a chill October morning like this one was preferable to the rest of the day, which would be spent doing what other people wanted of her. At nine o'clock, Adela would have lessons with her tutor, Dr. Sophus. After lessons would come lunch with her father, King Adalbert; her stepmother, Cecile; and her half-brother, Henry. Adela adored her father and four-year-old Henry, but Cecile never stopped talking. She tended to say whatever popped into her mind, and most of the time it had to do with Adela: *Now, dear, you really mustn't stuff yourself so — it isn't at all attractive. . . . Adela dear, I do wish you would remember to wear a hat outdoors. Your face is quite pink with sunburn.*

After lunch, Adela would have to suffer through two or three hours of embroidery instruction supervised by her stepmother, a torturous afternoon tea with the queen and her ladies-in-waiting, and then a dancing lesson. Cecile was determined to make a lady of Adela, and it did no good to complain about it, for Cecile was sure to mention the complaining at supper. At which point Adela's father would say, "You must listen to your stepmother. She knows what she's talking about."

This early in the morning, no one was ever about except for the palace servants and Adela. Her mother had died when she was born, and when she was small, Adela had done her best to escape from the various nannies and governesses her father had hired to care for her. Down to the kitchen for breakfast and then out into the garden. "Morning, my lass," the cook used to say when Adela was a girl. Now that Adela was seventeen, she still ate breakfast in the kitchen, but the cook's greeting had shifted to a more respectful, "Morning, Your Highness." Worse, she scolded the other servants when they forgot to curtsy to Adela.

This new deference was Cecile's doing. The queen had put a stop to what she called "lax and overly familiar behavior" from the servants when she had married King Adalbert five years ago. Cecile most certainly would have put a stop to Adela having breakfast in the kitchen had she known about it, but fortunately she didn't, and Adela trusted that the servants wouldn't say a word. She did wish the cook wouldn't scold the others, and she would have preferred that none of them curtsy, because, except for those formalities, she felt like she belonged with them, sitting quietly at the long wooden table, eating porridge and drinking coffee and listening to the kitchen gossip, which was always more interesting than the gossip at Cecile's afternoon tea.

The last weed was a dandelion, and Adela used her trowel to pry out the long root. She added the dandelion to the pile of weeds and stood up. She brushed off her smock and trousers and surveyed the result of her morning's work. Except for several patches of late-blooming daisies and black-eyed Susans, which she counted as wildflowers rather than weeds, this bed was cleared and ready for planting. Of course, the other flower beds still needed her attention, but that work would have to wait. It was nearly time for lessons.

"Miss Adela!"

Looking up, she saw Garth, the nineteen-year-old son of the head gardener, hurrying toward her. He was waving a piece of pink paper in the air and — what was that behind him? Of all things, a large magpie was hopping across the lawn! Adela stifled a laugh. "You're being followed," she called.

Garth glanced over his shoulder. "Stupid bird's been after me all morning," he said.

The magpie was greenish black with a white breast and a sharp black beak. Stark white stripes across the tops of its wings made Adela think of the epaulets on her father's military uniform. "He's rather handsome, isn't he?" she remarked.

"I never heard anybody call magpies handsome," said Garth. "Thieves is what they are. They'll steal just about anything."

"Look how he's watching us!"

"Miss Adela, I've received a letter!"

Garth was the only person outside her family who didn't say *Your Highness*. He had tried once not long after Cecile had married the king, and Adela had at first thought he was joking. "We've been friends all our lives! You've always called me Adela," she had told him.

"My father says I've got to be more respectful" had been his reply.

Adela suspected Cecile's influence, but Garth's

sense of duty to his father was so strong that they had settled on the compromise of *Miss Adela.*

"The letter was right outside our door this morning, on the front step," said Garth, who lived with his parents in a cottage at the edge of the palace grounds. "The handwriting's all fancy, and I couldn't make any sense of it."

Adela took the paper from him. "It smells like roses." She wrinkled her nose. "Too many of them!"

"Fairly makes my head swim," Garth agreed. "What's it say?"

Adela glanced at the signature, and her eyes widened in surprise. Then she read aloud, stumbling a bit because the handwriting was indeed difficult to decipher — lacy and overly elegant, and yet careless, with unexpected loops and tangles:

Dearest Garth,

You must come to see my garden. The roses are in bloom. All my flowers are in bloom: hyacinth, tulip, daffodil, chrysanthemum, calendula, bougainvillea, forget-me-not, lily, heliotrope, moonflower, columbine — I cannot name them all, there are so many. The scent is

heavenly. I hope I shall see you at my garden party this
coming Saturday at three o'clock in the afternoon.

    Hortensia

Adela looked up to see her own astonishment reflected in Garth's face.

"Is that the lady with the garden everybody talks about?" he asked.

Lady Hortensia was said to be a person of high rank—fabulously beautiful and fabulously wealthy. Her garden was rumored to be almost as beautiful as she was, with flowers of every kind and color, flowers that were constantly in bloom, flowers that never faded or died, as if winter never blighted their growth. Adela had never believed a word of it. The place sounded like something out of a fairy tale.

And yet here was a letter inviting Garth to come see it.

"People say her garden's magic," he said, sounding as if he believed what people said. Which was ridiculous, seeing as there was no such thing as magic. Still, not that many generations back—before Adela's great-great-great-grandfather, King Adalbert IV, had officially banned all belief in magic — most people had believed in it.

But during the reign of King Adalbert IV, the kingdom had been struck by a terrible earthquake that had killed hundreds of people, destroyed thousands of homes, and nearly shaken the royal palace from its foundation. In its aftermath, the king had summoned his royal magician to the throne room, demanding to know why the man had not been able to prevent or even predict the disaster. After the magician had offered feeble excuses, the king had denounced him as a charlatan and declared an end to the ridiculous and useless practice of magic.

In these modern times, there was still a royal magician at court. The person occupying this honorary position had but one duty: setting off fireworks at a midsummer event that commemorated the banning of magic and celebrated the triumph of science and reason over ignorance and superstition. The fireworks were supposed to represent false magic. At the end of the display, the royal philosopher would come forward, seize the royal magician's fake magic wand, and break it in two while shouting, "Only gunpowder!

Only gunpowder!" Adela's great-uncle Emeric had held the title of royal magician (along with several far more important ones) for years, and he was so old now that he had servants set off the fireworks. There was nothing magical about any of it.

All the same, you could still find people who clung to old beliefs — people willing to pay out a few pennies for a good-luck charm, people who believed in witches, love potions, and curses. Such gullible souls — Garth among them, apparently — might well believe some bizarre tale about a magic garden.

Feeling slightly embarrassed for her friend, Adela said only, "I imagine people must exaggerate a little, though I expect the garden is pretty enough. . . ."

And yet, even as she said it, Adela wondered how that could be true. How pretty could any garden be at this time of year? And, more to the point, where *was* Hortensia's garden? Adela felt she knew the location of every important garden in the kingdom. And she had visited all the ones close to home.

Or at least she thought she had. "Lady Hortensia doesn't tell you how to get to her garden," she said, looking at the letter again.

"There was a return address on the envelope," said Garth. "It said Flower Mountain. I did manage to puzzle that much out."

"I've never heard of it," said Adela. "Do you suppose it's in the Southern Mountains? It can't be much warmer there than it is here. How can all these flowers be blooming? Do you suppose she has a greenhouse?"

As of this summer, the royal palace had a new greenhouse. Adela, who had read extensively about these innovative glass buildings, had advised Garth's father on its design. She had even helped build it, ignoring Cecile's objection that carpentry wasn't a suitable occupation for a princess. There was still plenty of room in the greenhouse for new plants. Perhaps Hortensia would let Garth bring some home.

"Why do you suppose she's asking me?" he wondered.

"Because she knows you like gardening," said Adela.

Garth looked worried. "But won't it be a fancy kind of party? Why, I won't know what to do or say!"

Poor Garth! He had always been shy, apt to get tongue-tied around other people. He was especially uncomfortable around women, which was surprising, given that he was more than uncommonly handsome.

His sun-blond hair, bright-blue eyes, and strong arms were the talk of every servant girl in the palace. Even Adela, who very much thought of him as a friend and nothing more, lately found herself blushing when he smiled at her.

"You'll be fine," she told him. "We'll just have to dress you up a bit. You can borrow some clothes. I'm sure one of the footmen would be glad to lend you something."

Garth looked aghast. "You mean I'd have to dress up like that? Satin and lace and . . . and silk stockings and all?"

"You can't very well wear a gardener's smock and trousers."

He gave a groan. "I'm sure to look like an ass! And act like one, too!"

"You will not! Besides, most of the time you'll be wandering around, looking at beautiful flowers. That's what I would do if I were going!"

"I wish you *were* going. Say, Miss Adela, do you think maybe you could? I'd feel better if you were there."

Adela hesitated. It was of course rude to show up uninvited to a party. On the other hand, she was aware that certain rules of etiquette didn't fully apply to the nobility. People were generally flattered to have royalty attend their parties, and Hortensia would doubtless feel the same way. Oh, but Adela hated that sort of thing! She hated parties . . . people fawning all over her because she was a princess.

But the prospect of visiting a greenhouse full of exotic new plants was enticing. "All right, I'll go," she said.

Garth rewarded her with a smile, which, not unexpectedly, made her blush and look away. It was then that she saw the magpie staring up at her with its head cocked to one side. "Look at him!" Adela said with a laugh. "It's as if he's listening to us!"

Garth stomped his foot. "Get away, you!"

The bird screeched and took off into the air.

"Good riddance," said Garth. He took the invitation from Adela's hand and sniffed it tentatively. "People say Lady Hortensia's very beautiful," he commented, and then sniffed it again, this time breathing deeply.

"I hope she'll let us take some plants home," said Adela.

"Are you sure she won't think I'm an idiot?" asked Garth.

"Just some seedlings and cuttings — surely she can't mind. Oh, no! What time is it?"

"Quarter past —"

But Adela was already running toward the palace. "I'm late for lessons!" she called back. "And no! She won't think you're an idiot!"

chapter 2
DR. SOPHUS

Adela found her tutor, Dr. Sophus, in the library, sitting near the end of a long table covered with neat piles of books. He was middle-aged, thin, and wiry. His gray hair was clipped close, as was his beard. His eyebrows were thick and bristly above his dark eyes. He glanced up as she hurried into the room. "I see that you have spent your morning studying botany again."

Adela looked down at herself, relieved that her gardening clothes were relatively clean. "I didn't have time to change," she explained. "But I have scrubbed my hands."

She held them up for his scrutiny, and Dr. Sophus nodded. In addition to being Adela's tutor, he was also the royal librarian. He was fiercely protective of his books and disapproved of dirty hands.

"We'll pick up where we left off yesterday." He motioned toward the chair opposite his own. "Algebra, wasn't it?"

"I was wondering if we might start with geography," Adela suggested. She enjoyed algebra, but the puzzle of Hortensia's garden was on her mind. She told her tutor about the garden-party invitation. "Have you ever heard of Flower Mountain?" she asked.

Dr. Sophus, who loved maps almost as much as he loved books, was only too happy to deviate from the day's lesson plan. He crossed the room to a cabinet with deep shelves, each one only two inches high. He pulled out from one of these a map of the kingdom. "Not detailed enough," he decided after a moment's perusal. He put it back and pulled out another. The second map was larger and older, with yellowed edges, faded colors, and old-fashioned handwritten labels. Dr. Sophus traced his finger across the jagged range of mountains lying just to the south of the royal city: Fire Mountain, Evergreen Mountain, Mount Adamantine.

Adela leaned over her tutor's arm and spotted Flower Mountain at the same moment he did.

"Not quite in the kingdom, not quite out of it," said Dr. Sophus. "Right on the border."

"I'd never heard of it before today," said Adela.

"Nor I." Dr. Sophus looked somewhat bothered by this admission. It was rare that he came across something he didn't know. "What did you say this woman's name is?"

"Lady Hortensia," said Adela. "And her garden's supposed to be gorgeous. Flowers blooming all year round, never fading, never dying. Some people think it's *magic*."

"Really?" Dr. Sophus looked intrigued.

"I think it's more likely she has a greenhouse."

"Possibly." But Dr. Sophus's tone suggested that he thought otherwise.

Adela laughed. "Don't tell me you believe in magic, too!"

Her tutor gave a shrug. "I don't know whether believing has anything to do with it. After all, history is filled with references to magic. I am thinking, of course, of King Ival."

Adela was surprised. King Ival was one of her more

illustrious ancestors. His ancient sword and shield were on display in the throne room. A complicated family tree on the wall of her father's study showed how he was related to her, but she had never had the patience to count the two dozen or so *greats* that separated them in time.

"Any good history book written before the time of King Adalbert IV will tell you of King Ival's exploits," said Dr. Sophus. "You know what I mean — killing dragons, knocking the heads off trolls, frustrating the devious plans of evil witches and sorcerers . . ."

"Those stories aren't history," said Adela. "They're legends people have made up about King Ival because he was so famous." She had grown up reading those legends. They were highly entertaining, perfect subject matter for the many tapestries adorning the walls of the palace. One such tapestry hung in the library, and she looked up at it now. There was Ival, caught in the act of beheading a seven-headed dragon. Five heads were sliced off already; they lay on the floor of a room in a castle that belonged to a wicked sorcerer. Adela, who was familiar with the story, knew that Ival would cut off the remaining two heads, wrest open the iron cupboard behind the dragon, and try to drink from a flask he would find inside.

"Those are fairy tales," she told Dr. Sophus.

"So we have been advised. On the other hand, I have found it useful in my long life to keep an open mind about such things."

The thoughtful look on her tutor's face awoke a memory in Adela's mind. It was years ago; she had just begun having lessons with Dr. Sophus, and she had been so young that the bedtime stories about King Ival she loved so much still seemed real to her. It had been a shock to learn about King Adalbert IV and the banning of magic. "But where did all the magic go?" she had asked Dr. Sophus. "All the dragons and trolls and witches and sorcerers and everything?"

Her tutor had smiled. It was something he rarely did; he had a gentle, serious sort of face that didn't usually need to smile. "Well, Your Highness, if we are to believe your history book, those things never really existed in the first place. If we are to believe King Adalbert IV, there never was any magic."

"But what about King Ival?" Adela had asked, thinking of all the stories and the tapestries. "That's history, isn't it?"

Dr. Sophus had tilted his head, as if conceding her point. "Perhaps King Ival killed off all the dragons and witches and sorcerers."

"So there aren't any left! And there isn't any magic anymore!" This conclusion had been more satisfying to her young mind than the assertion that magic had never existed in the first place. It was only when Adela was older that she knew Dr. Sophus must have been teasing.

Except, she thought now, Dr. Sophus never teases anyone. Can he really believe in magic?

"Do you know what I think, Dr. Sophus?" said Adela. "I think Father ought to make you the royal magician instead of Great-Uncle Emeric."

Her tutor made a face. "An honor I would most certainly decline, Your Highness, seeing as I have never been fond of that midsummer event at which the royal philosopher breaks the royal magician's wand in two. Perhaps you will agree with me that, despite the fireworks, the ceremony is somehow a trifle . . . disappointing."

I suppose I do, thought Adela.

chapter 3
CECILE

"Good news!" the queen announced to the king at supper that evening. "The dancing master tells me that Adela has nearly mastered the minuet."

Hardly, thought Adela. She was a terrible dancer — always stepping on her teacher's toes, always going left when he went right. She didn't even like dancing.

"Given that she can already waltz, I think she'll be ready for her grand ball any day now," said Cecile.

Adela suppressed a groan. The grand ball was an idea her stepmother had been promoting for months. Her plan was to invite as many marriage prospects as possible so that Adela could, in Cecile's words, *look them over.* "You're seventeen and not getting any younger," her stepmother had pointed out. "Your mother was sixteen when she married your father, and I was eighteen. You're a lucky girl. I didn't get to have a grand ball."

By this Cecile meant that she had not been a princess; she was the daughter of a cloth merchant, and as a commoner, she couldn't have expected such a thing as a grand ball. But Cecile *had* been lucky in her marriage, for she had caught the king's eye when he was out riding one afternoon, a chance encounter that had led to the prize of a royal marriage proposal. "I'm as common as they come," the queen was fond of saying, "but true love doesn't care about such things."

Common would have been just fine with Adela. Only her stepmother had taken to her *uncommon* life with great relish. It was as if she had combed Dr. Sophus's library for books about how to be a queen: how to talk down to servants, how to speak as an equal to dukes and duchesses, how to find a suitable husband for one's stepdaughter. Adela was sure the idea for the grand ball could only have come out of a book.

"I don't want to get married," she had told Cecile.

"Of course you do!"

"No, I really—"

"Silly! Are you afraid no one will love you?"

"No, I—"

"Because you could be such a pretty girl, Adela! If you would only pay more attention to your hair and your skin, your clothing and how you carry yourself. All of these things *matter*."

What Adela had wanted to say was that she didn't want to get married *now*. That she had a thousand things she wanted to do before she even thought of getting married. She wanted to design elaborate and beautiful gardens. She wanted to travel to new places to learn new gardening methods, to collect plants she had never seen before, to bring them home and try to make them grow. But she'd had a hard time putting her dreams into words, especially to her stepmother.

"You can always garden," Cecile had told her. "It's a lovely hobby for a young woman."

"It's not a hobby!"

"Of course it's a hobby!" Cecile seemed unable to fathom that others might not agree with her ideas. Arguing with her had yet to get Adela anywhere, though she frequently forgot and tried anyway. The best thing to do was smile back as if she agreed and make other plans in secret.

Or change the topic.

That was the best tactic to use now, Adela decided. She cleared her throat. "I was wondering if I might borrow the carriage this Saturday. There's a party I'd like to attend. It's being given by Lady Hortensia."

She hadn't expected her father or stepmother to recognize the name, so Cecile's response startled her: "Lady Hortensia! Why, her garden party was all the talk at tea this afternoon."

Adela hadn't been at tea. She had come to lunch from her morning with Dr. Sophus still dressed in her gardening clothes, and her stepmother had insisted she use the time reserved for tea to have a bath and dress for her dancing lesson.

"Marguerite has also been invited," said Cecile.

Marguerite was the queen's younger sister and also one of her ladies-in-waiting. Marguerite was pretty, even more beautiful than Cecile. She was also, in Adela's opinion, extremely boring. She seemed to have no other interests besides fashion and men, and her knowledge of flowers extended only to the bouquets she received from her many male admirers. Why would Lady Hortensia have asked *her* to the same garden party as Garth?

"How splendid that you've been invited as well!" said Cecile. "You and Marguerite can travel together. I had thought I might need to go — as chaperone, you know — but that won't be necessary now. Just as well. I wouldn't want Lady Hortensia to think I was inviting myself."

"Indeed," Adela murmured, tucking into her supper with renewed focus.

"You and Marguerite can spend the day together."

Adela could imagine few things less appealing.

"And I can have the fun of helping you both get ready!" Cecile added.

Then again, maybe she could think of one thing.

chapter 4
KRAZO

In a walled yard in the center of Hortensia's garden grew a rose tree, with roses so red they looked as if they might bleed if anyone dared to pluck them. But no one ever did, for the thorns on that tree were as sharp as dragon claws. Under the rose tree was a white marble couch, and it was here, lying on a bed of soft, velvet cushions, that Hortensia liked to spend her afternoons. She liked to sleep there, soothed into drowsiness by the soporific scent of her roses.

On the afternoon of the day after Garth and Marguerite received their invitations, however, Hortensia was wide awake, firing questions at the magpie standing on the grass beside her.

"So? You delivered all the invitations?"

"Yes," said the magpie.

"And everyone is coming?"

"Yes."

"Including this princess! Do you really mean to say that she has invited herself?"

"Yes."

"Of all the presumption! If I had wanted her, I would have asked her! What does she look like?" Before the magpie could answer, Hortensia stopped him with a wave of her hand. "Never mind! If she were the least bit pretty, I would have heard of her. I'm sure she's as plain as a turnip blossom. I don't know what I'll do with the wretched creature. I suppose I'll have to start a kitchen garden." She let out a noise of disgust, threw herself back against the cushions, and closed her eyes.

The conversation might have been finished, or it might not. The magpie had no way of knowing, and so he waited.

His name was Krazo. Or at least that was what Hortensia called him. *Krahhh-zo! Krahhh-zo!* she would say, mocking his raspy voice. He had been Hortensia's servant for as long as he could remember. How long was that? It might have been ten years or a hundred;

Krazo had no idea. What had he done before his life with Hortensia began? Where had he lived? Again, Krazo had no idea. His past was such a dim place that he never thought of it, not even in dreams. His mind was strongly connected to the present, to that suspenseful moment linked to the future by the question *What will happen next?*

Hortensia was a demanding mistress, and Krazo was at her beck and call both night and day. It was primarily magic that bound him to her. She was a witch, and he must obey her commands or she would punish him. But there was also the fact that she glittered. Just now, for example, the magpie's eyes were kept busy by the sparkle of her adornments. Her flame-colored dress was embroidered with gold threads and amber beads. A gold collar set with amethysts circled her neck, a string of pearls wound through her dark hair, and rings decorated every one of her fingers — diamonds and emeralds, and rubies as big as berries. Hortensia loved jewelry.

So did Krazo. He knew that Hortensia had great quantities of jewelry in her bedchamber. But that was nothing compared to the treasure buried beneath the rose tree.

Late one night, some years past, Krazo had seen Hortensia enter the garden alone. Curious, he had followed her to this very spot, where he had watched her take a silver box out of her sleeve. After unlocking the box with a small silver key from a chain around her neck, Hortensia had sat there in the moonlight, gazing upon its contents. Krazo had not been able to see what was inside the box, but he knew it must be treasure, for Hortensia had locked it back up and buried it, tamping down the soil so that no one would ever guess it was there.

If Krazo could have dug up the treasure, he would have done so. But magpies, even talking ones, have their limits, and one of those is an inability to dig holes. Not that this prevented him from thinking about it. He was thinking about the buried treasure now, in fact, when suddenly Hortensia gave a low chuckle. Krazo looked up to see a smile playing at her lips. "It occurs to me," she murmured without opening her eyes, "that no matter how plain our princess is, she'll be sure to come to the party wearing all sorts of pretty baubles. Royals never skimp on their jewelry." Then she yawned, exhibiting a mouth full of perfect white teeth. She settled into her cushions. Presently she began to snore. Hortensia always snored when she slept, and it always jangled Krazo's nerves. The magpie was sensitive to sounds, both good ones and bad, and so, relieved to escape this particularly dreadful one, he made his departure.

He flew off to his nest, thinking about the princess.

Or, to be exact, he was thinking about the jewels she would wear.

chapter 5

PARTY PREPARATIONS

"What does one wear to a garden party?" was the first thing out of Marguerite's mouth at the next day's tea.

"Light colors," said Cecile. "Pale green, very light pink—actually, you might think about wearing a gown of mine. What about that lemon-colored dress with the lace trim?"

So it begins, thought Adela, watching the two sisters lean toward each other.

"Oh, Cecile! Would you really let me?" Marguerite was so excited that she had to set down her cup and saucer.

"Of course, darling. We'll just need to have the seamstress take the sides in a little. I declare you must have the tiniest waist in the kingdom."

"What should Her Highness wear?" asked Marguerite. "Wouldn't it be fun if we could dress in similar colors? You have that lovely peach-colored gown."

Cecile shook her head. "I'm afraid it would never fit her," she said, leaving unspoken the implication that Adela did *not* have the tiniest waist in the kingdom. Nor would she ever have a small waist, Cecile made clear with a hard look, if she continued taking pieces of cake from the tea tray. "Besides," added Cecile as Adela took a strawberry instead, "the color would wash out her complexion. No, I think as far as Adela goes, we'll have to settle for blue. You know what I mean, Marguerite — a nice forget-me-not blue."

"Her Highness has a silk gown in forget-me-not blue!" Marguerite exclaimed.

"Exactly! Though I do hope the silk won't be too heavy," Cecile commented. "Then again, our choices are limited, seeing as there isn't time to make anything new. Let's just hope it still fits her — Adela has grown so in the past year! But I suppose that's what a corset is for, isn't it?"

It was daring bit of humor for the queen, mentioning underwear at tea. Marguerite tittered appreciatively, as did the other ladies-in-waiting sitting around the table. Adela forced a smile and helped herself to more cake after all.

By Saturday morning, she was so tired of listening to Marguerite and Cecile, and so irritated by all the party preparations, that she almost wished she had never agreed to go.

The blue silk gown did fit her, though just barely. Adela's corset strings had to be pulled so tight, she could hardly breathe. Moreover, the skirt was too short, and there was no hem to let out. "You might try bending your knees a little," Cecile advised when she came into Adela's dressing room to view the results of their preparations.

"I might try not wearing these high-heeled shoes," Adela shot back. Her patience was wearing thin.

"Yes, dear, I know they're hard to walk in." Cecile's voice was indulgent. "But everyone looks at feet — they really do!"

"I should think they would want to look at the garden," Adela murmured.

"What do you think of Her Highness's hair, Cecile?" asked Marguerite, who had spent the last hour working with the hairdresser to achieve the creation that now topped Adela's head.

"I'm afraid to turn my neck," said Adela. "What if the pins come out?"

"I wonder if she should wear a tiara," said Marguerite.

"I am *not* wearing a tiara!"

Thankfully, Cecile agreed. "A tiara is a bit too formal, but we might think about a necklace."

Marguerite was already pawing through the jewelry collection Adela had inherited from her mother. "What about this?" She held up a diamond necklace that sent rainbows of light spinning across the walls and ceiling.

"Please, no!" said Adela. "I already look like a decorated cake!"

"There are earrings that match!" Marguerite said in a coaxing voice.

"*You* wear them."

"Why, Adela! What a thoughtful gesture!" said Cecile. "But you must wear *something*."

"What about sapphires?" said Marguerite, who was

already fastening the diamond necklace around her own neck. "To go with her sapphire gown."

Over the past few days, Adela's blue dress had been called *forget-me-not, cornflower, cerulean,* and *azure.* Now it was *sapphire.* Adela ducked her head and rolled her eyes. "I'll wear this," she said, fastening a pendant with a small blue stone around her neck.

"Small as it is, I suppose it will do," said Cecile. Then she stepped back to survey their appearance. She clasped her hands and exclaimed, "You are going to be the prettiest girls at the party!"

Overdressed and uncomfortable as she might be, Adela could only imagine how Garth must be feeling. He was standing beside the carriage when they came outside. He was wearing a footman's uniform: a dark-blue velvet jacket, crimson trousers made of satin, a white-ruffled shirt, and white silk stockings. His hair was combed and tied back with a red bow. He wore polished black shoes with shining silver buckles and heels almost as high as Adela's. Were his shoes giving him blisters, too? Adela wondered as she hobbled toward him.

"I've asked the cook to send along some lunch," said Cecile. "You can have a picnic along the way."

"I'm sure I won't be able to eat a morsel! I'm too excited," said Marguerite.

Just then Adela's ankle gave way, and she nearly tumbled. Garth jumped forward and caught her by the arm. Marguerite took her other arm. "Are you all right, Your Highness?" she asked.

"Adela, you really must be careful," Cecile chided. "That will be all, footman," she told Garth.

Oh, how awkward! Adela hadn't mentioned that Garth was coming to the party with them. It would be rude not to say something now. "Your Majesty, may I present Garth, the son of the head gardener," she said quickly. "He has also been invited to Lady Hortensia's party."

Cecile looked puzzled. Garth looked miserable. "M-m-much obliged, I'm sure, Your Majesty," he stammered. He bobbed his head in an approximation of a bow.

Marguerite gave a delicate cough.

"Garth, may I present Lady Marguerite?" said Adela.

Marguerite held out her hand. Garth was supposed to take it in his own, lean over it, and kiss the air directly above it.

Instead he turned red. He opened his mouth and made a small choking sound. He threw Adela an agonized look.

"Garth has a strong interest in gardens," she said helpfully.

"How lovely!" Marguerite withdrew her hand, and her face dimpled into a smile. "I love gardens, too. In fact, I've been told my name is a kind of flower."

Somehow Garth found his voice, nodding. "Sure enough, Miss Marguerite — your name's a kind of daisy."

Her eyes lit up with pleasure. "Why, you clever man! You must tell me everything you know about daisies."

"I — I will, Miss Daisy — I mean, Miss Marguerite — I mean, my lady," Garth stammered.

Marguerite held out her hand, and he helped her into the carriage. He helped Adela in as well. "Do you want to ride with us?" she asked.

He shook his head, looking almost frightened by the

suggestion. "I'll ride up top," he said as he closed the door. The carriage swayed as he climbed up beside the coachman. There was a grinding of wheels, and they lurched forward.

"Good-bye, girls!" cried Cecile.

Marguerite waved her handkerchief out the window and threw several kisses before falling back against the cushions. "My goodness! Did you ever see such a *handsome* man in your life? Your Highness simply must tell me everything about him!"

"He's the son of the head gardener," Adela repeated, sure that Marguerite must have missed this detail. Servants like Garth, even handsome ones, had never merited Marguerite's attention before. But she was surprised to see color blooming in Marguerite's cheeks, and even more surprised to see that Marguerite looked both shy and exultant at the same time.

"Oh, Your Highness! I'm sure he was flirting with me!"

"Garth?"

"Calling me Daisy like that," Marguerite elaborated. "Oh, I know it was fresh of him, but, really, I don't mind. Did you see how nervous he was around me?"

"Well, yes." Adela wasn't sure how to let on that Garth was nervous around practically everyone.

"Oh, Your Highness, *do* say you think he might care for me."

"Well, I—"

"I'm sure he must!" Marguerite spoke with certainty. The fact was that men were always falling in love with her. At least that was how it sounded from Cecile's afternoon teas, where Marguerite's romantic life was one of the queen's favorite conversation topics. Usually it was some dashing young captain who had danced every dance with Marguerite at a party, or a particular knight with a nice-looking mustache who had stared at her all afternoon at a tournament, or a foreign ambassador who kept writing her love letters long after his state visit was over. How funny it was to hear her going on now about Garth, of all people.

"Really, Marguerite," Adela began, trying not to laugh. "I—"

"I shall walk with him at the party," Marguerite decided. "You said he likes gardens! I shall walk with him and ask him questions about the flowers! Men love to be asked questions. It puts them at ease. Oh, but I'm sure *I* won't be at ease at all—not if he looks at me again with those eyes. Did you see how blue they were? Just like great big . . . great big . . ." Marguerite struggled for the right word.

"Forget-me-nots?" Adela suggested. "Sapphires?"

"Yes!" gushed Marguerite.

chapter 6
PICNIC LUNCH

It was well after noon when they stopped for lunch. The coachman pulled the horses over beside the dusty country road, and Garth helped Adela and Marguerite out of the carriage.

Adela stretched as best she could in her tight dress. Two hours of being cooped up in a carriage with chatty Marguerite had been almost more than she could stand, especially coming as it did after three full days of listening to Marguerite and Cecile put forth their various ideas about garden-party fashions. Never mind all that now, Adela told herself. Today would be the start of something new. She was going to collect new plants from Hortensia's garden. And it wouldn't be long before she would travel and visit other gardens. Not only that, she would explore woodlands and meadows, mountains and deserts. She was going to bring home plants nobody had ever seen before.

She looked around. What a fine spot for a picnic! A grove of birches with quivering leaves just beginning to turn yellow, lichen-covered boulders set among the trees like chairs, and, above everything, the mountains, stark and silent against the blue sky. Their dark forested slopes seemed to promise adventure. The sort you might find in a King Ival story, thought Adela. Not the sort you would expect to find at a garden party, which, no matter how much you liked flowers, was sure to be a rather tame event. "How much farther to Flower Mountain?" she asked.

The coachman—whose name, Axel, was a source of amusement for her father (*My coach has three axles,* the king would joke)—scratched his bald head and squinted up at the mountains. "My guess is we have at least another hour ahead of us, Your Highness. Hard to say, though, what with mountain roads being so unpredictable. Lucky for us there *is* a road—if you can believe the map, that is."

"We'd better eat quickly, then," said Adela. Hortensia's invitation had said three o'clock, which was rather late in the day for an outdoor party in autumn. Suppose they arrived even later and there wasn't time to see anything. "I'll hand out the food," she offered as Garth set the picnic basket down on the ground. She opened the lid to find cold chicken, cucumber sandwiches, lemonade, and sugar cookies. There were also china plates, crystal cups, and embroidered linen napkins. Adela was surprised that Cecile hadn't ordered the cook to send along a pair of gold candlesticks! "Who's hungry?"

Marguerite, settling herself on one of the boulders, politely declined. "Nothing for me, thank you, Your Highness. I had a bit of toast at breakfast."

"More for the rest of us," said Adela, who was famished in spite of having eaten toast, eggs, bacon, and pancakes earlier. "Here you go, Axel," she said, handing the coachman a plate piled with food, a cup filled with lemonade, and a napkin. She filled another plate and cup for Garth, then helped herself.

To her surprise, Garth sat down next to Marguerite. Oh, no! thought Adela. He can't possibly know what's to come. Marguerite had talked all morning about her plans for winning Garth's affection. Now Adela wasn't sure whether to laugh or feel sorry for him.

Sure enough, Marguerite set to work right away, smiling shyly and asking if Garth wasn't *terribly* excited about the party.

Blushing, he stammered that indeed he was.

"I *love* flowers," said Marguerite. "I *absolutely* love them. Don't you?"

Garth, still blushing, acknowledged that he did.

I suppose it won't hurt him to suffer now, thought Adela, but I'll have to sneak him away from her at the party. I'm a poor friend if I can't do that much.

She ate a chicken leg and wiped her fingers. Then she ate two cucumber sandwiches, sipped her lemonade, and thought about gardens.

"It's the knack for planning that makes the gardener," Garth's father had once told her. "You and my son both know what to do when it comes to the care and nurturing of flowers, Your Highness. I've taught you when to plant, when to prune, and so on. But I'll be the first to admit that Garth hasn't got an eye like you have—an eye that can see what you want before it all comes into bloom." It was a bit of praise that had made Adela's heart swell with happiness. She did love to plan a garden, and Hortensia's was sure to be a marvel of planning. She must have a great variety of fall-blooming flowers, thought Adela. And I can ask her what bulbs she's planted for the spring.

At that moment her ears picked up the sound of Marguerite's honey-sweet voice. "Do you really mean to say that some flowers—what did you call them, *pennials?*—come up year after year, all by themselves?"

"*Perennials*," said Garth, "and yes, they do."

"How marvelous!" exclaimed Marguerite. "And *daisies*, are those *pentennerals?*"

"Well, now, some are and some aren't."

"I suppose I could be a *pentenneral*, seeing as I am a kind of daisy."

"Yes, Daisy—I mean, my lady."

Marguerite dimpled. "I like it when you call me Daisy. You must always call me that."

Clearly embarrassed, Garth ducked his head. But he looked up quickly enough, a stupid grin on his face. "All right, then . . . Daisy."

Adela frowned. Was it possible that Garth actually

liked Marguerite? She watched his eyes follow the movement of Marguerite's hand as it fluttered up to tuck a curl back in place, brushed against the diamond necklace at her throat, then dropped to her waist, where it paused to smooth the fabric of her dress. Then Garth looked up, and his eyes met Marguerite's. They smiled at each other, and Adela felt as if she were spying.

He *does* like her, she thought. Or anyway, he likes to look at her.

Marguerite had wavy golden hair, blue eyes, and petal-pink cheeks. She was more than pretty; she was as lovely as sunlight. "I should love to plant a garden someday," she said.

Adela couldn't imagine anything more unlikely than Marguerite with a shovel in her hand.

"I could help you," said Garth.

"Oh, would you?"

I don't know why Marguerite looks so surprised, thought Adela. It's exactly what she wanted him to say.

"Do you know . . . ?" Marguerite's voice became tentative. "I — I was hoping that today you might walk with me at the party. I was hoping you might talk to me about gardening. You know so much, and I know so little!"

"Of course I will."

So much for wanting to protect Garth from Marguerite, thought Adela. He's practically throwing himself at her! Not that I care, she told herself quickly. It isn't as if he promised to look at Hortensia's garden with me.

But there was the rub: she did care.

It wasn't as if she had ever wanted Garth to look at her the way he was looking at Marguerite. But she *had* counted on his friendship. And it did seem unfair that someone as empty-headed as Marguerite could take it away so easily.

Stop it, Adela told herself. Garth is still your friend. And Marguerite *is* pretty. I suppose he can't help being attracted to her, any more than she can help being attracted to him. They do look nice together.

Now she sounded like Cecile, who was always saying things like, *Don't they make a handsome couple?* And, *Surely she can do better than that. He's not half as good-looking as she is!* As if people should be matched up by their looks, like the horses that pulled the royal carriage.

I would rather find somebody who's interesting than somebody who's handsome, thought Adela. It was funny, but whenever she had thought about Cecile's grand ball (not that she had thought about it much), it had never occurred to Adela that any of the men Cecile would invite might actually *be* interesting. What if one of them had a sense of humor, for example? What if one of them was brave and adventurous like King Ival? Would she be quite so set against marriage if she met a man who not only encouraged her to follow her dream of traveling but would even ride alongside her when she did?

I suppose I might choose that man, Adela decided. If I *wanted* to marry someone.

But what if he didn't want to marry her? What if he didn't think she was pretty enough? Because she wasn't pretty—not really—no matter how much Cecile insisted that she could be if she tried harder. Adela's nose, for example, was a little too large for her face, and her mouth a little too wide. Her hair was long and sand-colored and unrelentingly straight.

Moreover, she was very tall—taller than most men, including Garth. She was so tall that Cecile was taking her height into account in assembling the guest list for the grand ball. "Don't worry, dear! We'll be sure to invite a few tall marriage prospects for you," she had said recently.

And Adela's father had added, "I shouldn't worry too much, Cecile. What does it matter how tall she is or what she looks like? She's the king's daughter. Who isn't going to want to marry her?"

Which had hurt a bit, actually, and Adela had been forced to remind herself that she didn't want to get married. She wanted to be a gardener—a *real* gardener, not someone who practiced it as a hobby.

"What do you think, Your Highness?" said Marguerite just then, startling Adela out of her thoughts. "Don't you agree that Garth should ride inside the carriage the rest of the way?" Marguerite gave Garth a sidelong smile.

"Of course," said Adela.

As they packed up the picnic things, she considered how lucky she was that no one would ever look at her the way Garth was looking at Marguerite. The way people looked at a flower. Think what a distraction it would be, she told herself. I would never get any gardening done at all!

Only it did make a person feel a bit lonely, watching two other people fall in love.

chapter 7

DIAMONDS

A magpie's nest is a messy-looking thing, and Krazo's was as messy as they come, with twigs poked together in a bowl shape and a twig roof over the top. He had built it in a spruce tree on the front lawn of Hortensia's estate.

It was here that he kept his treasures. These consisted of an emerald brooch, a gold watch set with paste diamonds, a turquoise-and-silver bracelet, a little pearl ring, and Krazo's favorite piece, a flashy belt buckle studded with amethysts and garnets. Over the years, these prizes had been left behind by party guests. Usually Hortensia was attentive when she collected "the loot," as she called it, but every so often she overlooked something. That was a lucky day for Krazo.

On the day of the garden party, Krazo woke up feeling lucky. More guests than usual would be attending this party, and he had high hopes that Hortensia might overlook something that afternoon. He also felt free for the day; Hortensia always slept late, and she rarely called for him during one of her parties. The magpie spent the morning arranging the treasures he already owned, getting things ready for the new ones he hoped to acquire. He hung the pearl ring on a twig poking out of the wall, draped the watch over another twig, and pushed the turquoise bracelet into the middle of the nest, where it caught the light from one of two entrances. Then he changed his mind — the bracelet was sadly tarnished — and he pushed the belt buckle into the light instead.

As he worked, Krazo thought about the guests who would be coming to the party. Not all of them would bring treasures. The young men, for example, really couldn't be counted on. Except for kings and dukes and princes (and there would be none of those today), men didn't wear much jewelry. But there would be plenty of young ladies at the party, and Hortensia had been speculating about what they might bring for days. "The little dairymaid won't have much in the way of jewelry," she had remarked, "though her parents may dig out an old locket or something. But she's as sweet as a primrose, so it hardly matters." Then there were the twin sisters Hortensia had invited. "Red hair, freckles on their noses — adorable creatures," Hortensia had commented. "Their father is a sea captain. Sea captains are always bringing their wives and daughters pretty things." There was also a shopgirl coming to the party; Hortensia thought she might borrow something from the shop where she worked. And last but not least, there were the princess and the other young lady from the royal court. Krazo didn't need Hortensia to tell him that royals always came loaded down with jewelry. His emerald brooch, for instance, had belonged to the daughter of a duke, as had his pearl ring. The duke's daughter had come to one of Hortensia's parties wearing bracelets all the way up her arms, gold chains around her neck, and rings on her fingers. Small wonder Hortensia had overlooked the brooch in that pile of treasure!

The important thing today, Krazo knew, would be

to put himself in the way of opportunity. And so, as the sun began to crawl down the afternoon side of the sky, he made his way to the front lawn. A wisteria vine twined above the portico of Hortensia's palatial home, a vantage point that made it a perfect hiding place. He had just settled himself in among the fragrant blossoms when he spied a young man walking through the front gate. It was the gardener from the royal palace, and as he came up the drive, Hortensia came out to greet him. The gardener slowed, staring dumbly at her as most men did when they saw her for the first time. Krazo watched his mistress place her hand in the crook of the man's elbow. "Garth, isn't it? I've been so looking forward to meeting you. My garden is in the back. Come along and I'll show it to you." They strolled off, Hortensia's voice fading until the only sound was the quiet splash of the marble fountain in front of the portico.

Where was the princess? Krazo wondered.

He had his answer not five minutes later when a carriage rolled up the drive. The princess leaned out the window. "Stop beside the fountain, please, Axel!" she called to the coachman.

"Whoa!" The coachman pulled up on the reins and climbed down. The princess opened the carriage door, and the coachman helped her down.

Krazo leaned forward. He could see a necklace—a small blue stone. Was that all she was wearing?

Now the coachman was helping a second young woman out of the carriage. "Diamonds," Krazo muttered at the sight of her necklace. "Much better!"

"Where is Garth?" said the girl with the diamonds. "He promised to meet us."

"He was only going to walk ahead and see how much farther it was," said the princess. "It wasn't far. He must be nearby."

But what was this? Krazo saw that another girl was climbing out of the carriage. It was the dairymaid. She yelped as she stepped to the ground, and the princess rushed to her side. "How's your ankle, Bess?"

"It hurts something awful, miss," moaned the dairymaid. "I can't believe I twisted it!"

"It was lucky we saw you sitting beside the road. Here, let me help you to the fountain. You can soak your ankle in the water. It's cold and might keep the swelling down." The princess spoke in a soft voice that Krazo liked.

Then his gaze darted back to the girl with the diamonds. Krazo stared, fascinated, as she fingered her necklace. A moment later, she reached up to touch her earrings, one after the other.

And now more guests were arriving. Three people on horseback—the shopgirl and the other two men Hortensia had invited—were coming up the drive, and behind them another carriage. Krazo watched the young men dismount and jostle with each other to help the shopgirl down from her horse. He saw that she was wearing a string of pearls. He watched the ship captain's daughters climb out of the carriage. They were wearing necklaces of coral beads against their matching green gowns. Krazo's gaze flickered from one treasure to the next—pearls, coral beads, diamonds, and the princess's blue stone.

The guests were introducing themselves. "Where's the garden? Where's Lady Hortensia?" someone asked.

"The garden's probably behind the house. Perhaps she's there," said the princess.

"Maybe the stables are there, too," said her coachman.

Which made Krazo think of all that was about to

happen. The garden was behind the house, as was Hortensia, but there were no stables. Krazo knew that his mistress would deal with the two coachmen as she always did. Before the day was through, she would send them back down the mountain driving empty carriages. Of course, she would work her magic on them first: by the time the men reached home, they wouldn't remember much of anything about their day at Flower Mountain.

He watched the coachmen climb up on their carriages. He watched the horses start forward, following the graveled road that led around the house to the garden that was there, and the stables that were not. He watched the shopgirl, the twin sisters, and the two young men follow behind. There go the pearls and the coral beads, thought Krazo.

At any other time, he would have followed them, to see where in the garden they ended up. But today there were diamonds.

"We should go, too," said the princess. "Can you walk, Bess?"

The dairymaid pulled her bare foot out of the water. She stood up, took a hesitant step, and gave a sharp cry. She took another step, crumpled to the ground, and burst into tears. "Ow!" she cried. "How am I to see the garden if I can't walk? And I'm hungry. I haven't had anything to eat since I left home this morning."

Crying was something Krazo had observed many times at Hortensia's parties, and it always produced the same reaction in him: a sort of catch in his throat as if he'd choked on a fly. It wasn't a bad feeling exactly, but it wasn't pleasant, either. He felt the catch in his throat now and wondered, as he always did, what it was about crying that made him feel that way. He watched as the princess crouched down beside the dairymaid.

"You poor thing," she said. "There's sure to be food at the party. Why don't you lean on me and we'll go see. Or better yet, suppose I carry you!"

The dairymaid dried her eyes, and the catch in Krazo's throat went away, just as it always did when someone stopped crying. But this time, its disappearance was accompanied by a comfortable feeling — the sort of feeling he had when he went to sleep at night. Was it the soft voice of the princess that made him feel like that?

He watched her kick off her shoes and pull off her stockings. Then she dropped to one knee and presented her back to the dairymaid. "Climb on!" she commanded, and the next thing Krazo knew, the princess was standing up with the dairymaid on her back. She staggered forward. She was laughing—a sound Krazo liked even more than the sound of her speaking voice.

"Shouldn't we wait for Garth?" asked the girl with the diamonds.

"It's getting late! I want to see the garden before it gets dark!" said the princess. "Besides, poor Bess is famished!"

Krazo wanted to follow her. He had never seen anyone carry another person like that before. Like a horse, he thought.

"I really think we should wait," said the girl with the diamonds. "Garth told me he would meet me at the top of the mountain!"

But no one heard her except Krazo. The princess and the dairymaid were too far away.

"If Garth cares for me at all, he'll come find me," said the girl with the diamonds, her voice sounding uncertain. She sat down on the edge of the fountain, her back very straight, her body motionless. In less than a minute, Krazo was completely bored. Perhaps he should follow the princess after all.

And then the girl moved her hand. She touched her necklace again and touched her earrings, one after the other.

No, he decided. Treasure like this doesn't come very often.

Keep your eye on the diamonds, he told himself.

chapter 8
CORAL BELLS

For such a small person, the dairymaid was surprisingly heavy. Adela was panting and sweating by the time she rounded the back of Hortensia's house. Finding no one in sight, she guessed that the carriages had continued to follow the road she was on. She could see it turning at the end of a high stone wall. As for the other guests, they must have gone into the garden. She could see what must be the entrance, about halfway down the wall. She stumbled toward it, pebbles digging into her bare feet. "I'm going to have to put you down, Bess!" she warned as she entered the garden.

There was a ripping noise as the dairymaid slipped to the ground. "Oh, no! I've torn your dress!" Bess exclaimed.

But Adela didn't care. She was in the garden at last. There was a peony bush in front of her. Its blossoms were peach colored and twice as large as any she had ever seen before. In fact, the bush itself was larger than any she had ever seen.

Bess settled herself on the ground, her injured ankle stretched out in front of her.

"Did you ever hear of peonies blooming in the fall?" asked Adela.

"Never!" said Bess. "Nor lilacs. But that one's lovely, isn't it?"

The lilac tree leaning over the peony was also enormous, with creamy white flowers. "Lilacs bloom in the spring," said Adela.

"Everything's always in bloom in Hortensia's garden," said Bess. "It's magic."

Adela thought of the wisteria she had seen on the front lawn. Another springtime flower. Now she studied the flowers dotting the beds on either side of the cobbled path that led away from the entrance. Was that a daffodil . . . in October? She walked over to it, marveling at its teacup-shaped blooms, which were so large they were actually teacup-*size*. "And here's a chrysanthemum! I know they don't bloom at the same time as daffodils," she murmured. "I suppose Hortensia must move her flowers out of a greenhouse when they're ready to bloom. But what a lot of work! And how could she possibly move the lilac and the wisteria?"

"I think I'll wait here, if that's all right," said Bess. "Maybe you could bring me something to eat."

Adela nodded absently and wandered on. She turned a corner and found another path bordered with flowers. She walked along it, wondering at what she saw, until she turned another corner and found more paths to choose from. Before long, she was lost in a maze of winding paths running between walls too high to see over.

How different Hortensia's garden was from the gardens at home! The palace gardens had wide-open lawns and terraces — broad bands of colors and texture. But this garden felt closed in and secret, with surprises at every turn. The roses were astonishing. They were all different from one another: damasks, centifolias, china roses, tea roses, musk roses, and ramblers and scramblers that threw themselves up and over the walls. The roses can't have been moved from a greenhouse, Adela decided. Hortensia must have been cultivating them in the ground for years.

The other flowers were no less dramatic, in part because they were so large, but also because the rumors about Hortensia's garden were proved true: spring, summer, and fall flowers were indeed blooming at the same time. Here was a pink-and-white-striped carnation growing next to a sunny-yellow hollyhock. Here was a deep-purple heliotrope standing next to a bright-red poppy. And here was another poppy, this one blue, leaning over a lily of the valley with bell-shaped flowers the size of thimbles. How does Hortensia do it? Adela wondered.

Best of all was the rose tree. She found it in an enclosed yard where there were no other flowers to vie for her attention. The tree was twice as tall as she was, and the air around it was thick with the scent of its spectacular red flowers. Adela reached up to touch one of the blooms, caressing petals as soft as her brother Henry's little face. She closed her eyes, breathing in the fragrance. It wasn't until she opened her eyes that she noticed the thorns.

She stepped back. "Garth always says you can tell a rose by its thorns," she murmured.

She wondered if Garth had seen the tree. It was strange that she hadn't come across him. Stranger still that she hadn't met anyone at all. How long had she been walking?

Adela left the enclosed yard. She called out, "Hello? Hello!"

She listened. How quiet it was here! In the garden at home, there were always sounds — birds singing, bees humming, flies buzzing. And at this time of day, especially at this time of year, you would expect to hear a few crickets chirping.

Maybe the party was on the lawn or inside the house. But someone — Garth or Marguerite — ought to have come looking for her. . . . Adela let out a sigh of exasperation. Those two were so wrapped up in each other, they had probably forgotten she was here.

Purposefully, she started down the path in what she hoped was the direction of the garden entrance — or exit, as she now thought of it. She turned one corner after another until it occurred to her that the marble bench ahead of her looked familiar. Hadn't she already passed it once?

Adela sat down. I'm going in circles, she thought. I'm lost and nobody has thought to come find me. Marguerite and Garth are in their own little world. I don't blame Bess for giving up on me. But I hope Axel will think of me when it's time to go home.

Which it would be soon. The shadows were growing longer and the air cooler with the approach of twilight. Adela listened to the stillness, trying to think what to do, when something brushed against her hand. She looked down to see a cluster of pinkish-orange blossoms. There were other clusters, all of them rising up on tall stalks from a fat cushion of green and maroon leaves with scalloped edges. Coral bells, she thought, pleased with herself for recognizing the flower. There was an identical plant at the other end of the bench, the pair of them forming a pretty frame for anyone who sat there.

Then Adela looked closer. Draped among the leaves of one of the plants, almost hidden from sight, was a necklace, its coral beads the same color as the flowers.

"Coral bells and coral beads," she murmured. She had seen the twins wearing coral necklaces earlier. One of them must have dropped hers.

Adela untangled the necklace — a tricky job, for she didn't want to harm the plant. She had just pulled the beads free when she heard voices.

chapter 9
AN UNCOMMON DAISY

The voices were coming from the other side of the wall behind Adela.

"A pretty girl like you must have a string of admirers," said a woman's voice.

"I suppose there are a few," said the second voice, high and rather sugary.

Marguerite, thought Adela.

"I'm sure you're being modest," said the other woman. "I met a young man earlier today who I'm sure must be smitten with you."

"Really?"

"That nice young gardener . . ."

"You mean Garth! You saw him? Where?"

"I must say, he is every bit as handsome as I thought he would be," said the woman. "One hears about such things, you know."

What an odd thing to say, thought Adela. She had been about to call out, to announce her presence. But there was something not quite right about the unknown woman: Adela could hear it in her voice. Quietly, she climbed up on the bench, the marble cold against her feet. Standing on tiptoe, she could just see over the top of the wall. Yes, there was Marguerite in her yellow-and-white dress. She was looking up at the most beautiful woman Adela had ever seen.

"He *is* good-looking, isn't he! I only just found out that he likes me," said Marguerite. "He calls me Daisy," she added, blushing a little.

"Does he?" said the woman.

Is that Hortensia? Adela wondered. She isn't just beautiful; she's perfect.

"My name is a kind of daisy," said Marguerite.

"So it is," said the woman. "Such a common little flower. Don't you think most girls would rather be compared to, say, a rose?"

"I — I'm sure I don't know," said Marguerite.

"Then again, I imagine you are a rather common girl. Pretty enough to be sure, but hardly *rose* quality."

Marguerite looked as if she were trying to figure out whether the woman had intended to be rude.

"On the other hand, there isn't anything *wrong* with daisies," the woman continued. "And to tell the truth, I've never had one in my garden."

"It really is a lovely garden," said Marguerite, clearly eager to change the subject.

But the woman didn't seem to hear. She was walking around Marguerite, studying her.

"What is it?" Marguerite turned quickly, looking down at her skirt. "Is there something on my dress?"

"Daisy, it is!" said the woman, and she raised her hand. She made a graceful gesture in the air and began murmuring something; Adela couldn't hear what it was, but suddenly Marguerite gave a gasp. Her arms flew up in the air.

"What are you doing?" she cried as her yellow-and-white lace dress began to rustle and swirl about her. Though there wasn't the slightest breeze, the skirt was whirling around on its own, revealing Marguerite's lace petticoat and silk stockings. The petticoat and stockings ought to have been white, and Marguerite's high-heeled shoes ought to have been embroidered white satin. But now the petticoat and stockings and shoes were green. Adela was so distracted by this detail that it took her a moment to realize that Marguerite's legs and her feet were twisting and turning and digging themselves into the ground! Meanwhile, she was getting smaller. She gave a cry that was scarcely audible; her mouth had become a tiny little thing. Marguerite was now barely four feet tall and getting shorter by the moment. Her arms weren't arms anymore; they looked like pale-green stems. Marguerite's legs weren't legs anymore; they looked like stalks sprouting from the ground. And her lacy petticoat wasn't a petticoat; it was a frothy mass of green leaves. The yellow-and-white gown seemed to tear itself apart until there were a dozen tiny patches of yellow and white scattered among the leaves. Adela watched in horror as Marguerite's arms, now a darker green and sprouting yet more leaves, reached out imploringly to the woman. Marguerite's blond head grew smaller and smaller until it was nothing but a yellow center surrounded by a fringe of white petals.

Then everything was as quiet as it could be, and the

woman was standing there alone, looking down upon a plant as common as any that ever grew. Or perhaps not so common. The daisy, crowned with its cheery yellow-and-white flowers, was unusually large.

The woman leaned over to pick something up from the ground; Adela noted dully that it was the diamond necklace. The woman fastened it around her neck. There were already two other necklaces there — a string of pearls and a set of coral beads like the ones in Adela's hand. The woman adjusted the new necklace and, without another glance at the daisy, set off down the path.

chapter 10
THE CRYING WOMAN

Krazo could hardly believe his good fortune. There, not three hops from his hiding place under a sweetspire bush, lay a diamond earring. It looked like a chip of ice among the leaves of the daisy. Not only that, but he also knew that there must be another diamond earring hidden in the leaves. It was all he could do to keep himself from darting out to seize the treasure.

But it was best to be cautious. Hortensia might remember the earrings. She might come back. Better to give her time to get back to her house, where she would no doubt want to rest up in anticipation of the extravagant feast she would hold that evening. Hortensia always celebrated in grand style after one of her garden parties.

Keep your eye on the diamonds, Krazo had told himself earlier. And so he had stuck by the girl who was wearing them, forgoing the chance to acquire treasures from other guests. He had sat behind the wisteria vine, watching the girl grow more and more fretful, until at last Hortensia had shown up and invited her into the garden. He had followed along stealthily as Hortensia went through her usual round of questioning. *Looking for inspiration,* she always called it. *Not just any flower will do. It must be the right flower for the right girl.*

Which in this case meant a daisy with diamonds twined among its leaves.

Was it safe now? Could he snatch the earrings?

Just as Krazo was about to emerge from his hiding place, he heard a whimper from somewhere above him. "Marguerite?" someone whispered. There was a scraping noise and more whimpering, and then something came crashing down in front of him.

It was the princess. She straightened, looking up and down the path. "Marguerite?" she said, louder this time. "If this is some sort of trick, it isn't funny!"

Too loud! thought Krazo.

The princess looked as if she agreed; she seemed to shrink into herself as if she, too, feared the return of Hortensia. She tiptoed over to the daisy and reached out with a trembling hand to touch its blossoms and leaves. "Marguerite?" she whispered. Then she gasped, and Krazo saw her hand close around the diamond earring. She stared at it, then fell to her knees beside the daisy.

But what was that in her other hand? Coral beads? Where had she found those? Krazo was sure he had just seen Hortensia wearing them.

Then he remembered. There were two strings of coral beads: two sisters, two necklaces. Hortensia had taken one, but not the other, and the princess had taken it for herself.

Oh! Oh! This was too much! Now she was pushing aside the leaves of the daisy. She was looking for the other earring!

Krazo darted forward. The princess gave a cry of surprise as he bit down — hard — on her wrist.

"Ow!" she yelped. Krazo seized the earring in his beak and yanked it away. He skittered down the path, craning his head to see if the princess would follow.

When she did, he would rush back and get the other earring, too.

But she wasn't coming after him. Krazo slowed, and then he stopped.

The princess's wrist was in her mouth, and she was crying. Foolish girl! She wasn't even looking at the diamond! He could run back and grab it before she even noticed. He could grab the coral beads while he was at it.

But he didn't. For he could feel the familiar catch in his throat. And as the princess's tears went on, the catch in his throat grew worse. It became a pain in his breast.

Such a thing had never happened to him before. The girls he had seen cry had never cried this long. That was because Hortensia was changing them into flowers, and once that was finished, so was the crying. But now Hortensia was nowhere in sight, and Krazo was in agony; he felt as if an eagle's talons were ripping at his heart. He opened his beak to cry out, but he couldn't make a sound. A tremor ran through his body, and he closed his eyes.

Stop crying, he thought.

The princess didn't stop.

Stop crying!

And then a strange thing happened in his mind. He seemed to hear someone else crying as well. It was a woman. And — Krazo stumbled sideways — he could see her in his mind! She was sitting huddled on a rough stool in the corner of a foul little room, the stub of a tallow candle on a table next to her. The room was freezing cold. Krazo knew without knowing how he knew that this room was often cold because there wasn't enough money for a fire. He knew the woman, too. And he knew that someone had made her cry like that. Someone very close to her . . .

Who?

The pain in Krazo's breast was killing him, but still he asked himself the question.

Who?

He felt as if he should know the answer, if only he could remember.

Who?

And then the pain overwhelmed him, and his mind went dark.

chapter 11

AN UNEXPECTED CONVERSATION

Adela rarely cried. Perhaps that was why it was so hard to stop now. The tears kept coming, even as she wiped them away, even as she tried to convince herself that there was nothing to cry about. Nothing but a crazy magpie attacking her out of nowhere. As for the rest . . . "I must have imagined it," she whispered as she rubbed her eyes against her arm. And yet the grotesque vision in her mind would not go away: Marguerite twisting and turning into a daisy, as if by . . . as if by . . .

Resisting the word *magic*, Adela looked down at her hand. It was bleeding just below the thumb. She looked at the magpie. It had collapsed on the path a short distance away, a diamond earring clutched in its claw.

Which made her think of the other earring. There it was, tangled up in the leaves of the daisy. Carefully, Adela worked it free, watching the white-and-yellow flowers bob on their long stems, staring up at the sky the way daisies always did. *Day's-eyes,* Garth's father called them. "I must have imagined it," Adela whispered again. She closed her eyes and murmured a reassurance to herself: "Marguerite must have dropped the earrings. And the diamond necklace, too. That woman picked up the necklace, and here are the earrings, and poor Marguerite must be worried silly that she's lost them."

Poor Marguerite. It didn't matter that Adela's eyes were closed. For with those words, the vision rose up again in her mind—ridiculous and horrible, impossible and yet real, because, after all, she had seen it. Feeling tears coming on again, Adela gave a low moan.

"Don't cry!" said a voice.

"What?" Startled, she opened her eyes.

The magpie was on its feet again, its head tucked low, its plumage puffed out as if it were trying to keep warm. Adela saw it open its beak: "Don't cry!"

She shook her head. She really *was* imagining things.

The magpie shifted its head back and forth — fixing her with its left eye, its right eye, its left again. "Where is it?" asked the bird.

Adela gasped. "Are you — are you talking to me?"

"Give me the diamond!"

One of Cecile's ladies-in-waiting had a parakeet that could talk. The silly thing could say *Hello* and *Pretty bird,* but it couldn't carry on a conversation. Adela looked at the earring in her hand. She looked at the magpie. "Do you mean this diamond?" she asked.

"Give it to me!"

She sat up, as shocked as if she had been hit in the face with a bucket of water. The word she had resisted earlier came more easily now. "Are you — are you a *magic* bird?"

It lifted its head, stretched its wings out, and pulled them back in, smoothing its feathers as it did so. "I am a magpie!"

I am talking to a bird, thought Adela. But birds don't talk! Then again, she told herself, people don't get turned into daisies, either. Excited now, she said, "I saw that woman turn Marguerite into a flower. Did that really happen?"

"Give me the diamond!" said the magpie.

"That woman was Lady Hortensia, wasn't she? Can you tell me if she changed the others into flowers, too? You see, I found this, and I thought . . ." Adela held up the string of coral beads.

The magpie regarded the necklace with one black eye. "How many?" it croaked.

"How many? Well, there was Marguerite, and Bess, and those sisters, and that girl with the dark hair, and Garth, and —"

"How many *beads*?" said the magpie.

"B-beads?"

"On the string! How many beads on the string?" The magpie stretched out its neck and opened its black beak as if it wanted to eat them.

"What?" said Adela. "How should I know? What about the other guests? Do you know if any of them are left? Or did Lady Hortensia turn them into flowers, too?"

The magpie looked at her with its other eye. "Give me the necklace, and I'll answer."

Greedy thing, thought Adela. But she tossed the beads onto the grass between them.

The magpie seized them in its claw and dragged

them backward. "Yes," it said once it was a safe distance away.

"Yes, what?"

"Yes is the answer to the question," said the magpie.

"To which question?" Adela said in frustration. "I want to know if I'm the only one left!"

The magpie appeared to be counting the beads.

"Well, am I?" she demanded.

The magpie looked up. "Another question! Give me my diamond, and I'll answer."

"It isn't yours!"

The bird went back to counting, but Adela saw it steal a look at the diamond earring. She tossed it to him. "Did Lady Hortensia change all the guests into flowers?" she asked.

The magpie placed the new earring next to the other and said, "No."

Not all the guests . . . Did that mean Garth was safe?

"Who?" asked Adela. "Who did she change?"

"What else have you got?"

"What do you mean?"

"Treasure," said the bird.

It wanted more jewelry; it was looking at her necklace. Adela undid the clasp and held it out. The magpie's head waved back and forth as it followed the movement of the swinging chain. Adela pulled her hand back. "I want to know everything!" she said.

"I'll tell you what I saw."

She tossed the necklace onto the grass. "What? What did you see?"

The magpie grabbed the stone in its beak and pulled the necklace into its pile of jewelry. "I saw her change that girl into a flower."

"Which girl? Do you mean Marguerite?"

"Another question," said the magpie. "More treasure."

"I haven't got anything else!"

The bird gave her one of its sideways looks.

"I really haven't!" said Adela. "You have to tell me what happened."

But the magpie made an angry noise: *Ackkkk!* Then, as she watched, it looped the coral beads around its neck. It picked up her necklace in its beak, grasped an earring in each claw, and hopped once, twice, three times down the path before launching itself into the air.

"Wait!" cried Adela. "Come back!"

Too late! The magpie was gone.

chapter 12

AN OPEN MIND

It was dark by the time Adela found her way out of the garden.

By then she was tired and hungry and cold and—more than anything—filled with doubts. She couldn't help wondering if she might have dreamed it all. Who ever heard of a talking magpie? How could Hortensia have turned Marguerite into a daisy?

On the other hand, Adela couldn't help recalling Dr. Sophus's comment about keeping an open mind with regard to magic. Was it possible that Hortensia was some kind of witch? Adela tried to remember what she knew about witches in stories. Weren't they always old hags with green faces and warts? No, that wasn't true. Sometimes there were beautiful witches. King Ival had once faced one just like that. What if Hortensia was that kind of witch?

Until she knew for sure, Adela decided, it was best to be cautious.

She circled around to the front of the house and saw that there were lights on inside. Not only that, but she could also see shadows flickering on the walls. She could even hear muffled laughter. Hope quickened in her. Maybe she *had* imagined everything.

Resolute, she walked to the front door and raised her hand to knock. Then she thought better of it and tried the knob instead.

The door was locked.

She put her ear to the door, straining to hear what was going on inside. She couldn't pick out individual voices, only a lot of laughter — rather drunken laughter from the sound of it. People were having a good time. That was promising, wasn't it?

It was easy to believe that everyone was safe inside — Bess, Marguerite, and Garth — even if it wasn't exactly comforting that they had forgotten about her. Still, under the circumstances, being forgotten was preferable to having everyone turned into flowers.

Yes, Adela could almost believe that everything was fine.

Almost.

She decided that she needed to leave Flower Mountain. She would ride down the mountain, find the nearest village, and ask for help.

The trouble was that there didn't seem to be any horses to ride. Adela went back around the house and down the road she thought might lead to Hortensia's stables, only to find that it ended at a high stone wall.

Never mind, she decided. I'll walk down the mountain.

She returned to the front of the house. She found her shoes and stockings where she had left them beside the fountain. Tucking them under her arm, she ran barefoot across the lawn to the front gate.

But, to her dismay, the gate was locked. It was also much too high to climb: she tried, but the long vertical bars provided no foothold. The walls encircling the estate were also too high. When Adela had noticed them earlier in the day, she had assumed they were there to keep wild animals out. Now it seemed as if they were there to keep her in. She grasped the bars of the gate and stared at the road on the other side.

At last she turned back toward the house. The lights were still on. The shadows were still flickering on the walls. Adela had no doubt that the people inside were laughing and enjoying themselves.

What she could not afford to doubt — at least, not at the moment, when it was dark and she was alone and the gate was locked — was what she had seen earlier: a beautiful witch, a daisy that wasn't a daisy, and a talking magpie.

Best to keep an open mind, Dr. Sophus had said.

I'll hide, Adela told herself. I'll hide somewhere, and in the morning, I'll know if it was all a dream. I can decide what to do then.

There were no good hiding places on the lawn — only a few trees with branches too high to reach. No shrubs or beds of flowers. Adela's only choice was to head back into the garden, where she chose the first hiding place she could find: a rhododendron with white flowers that seemed to glow in the moonlight. Putting aside the thought that it might not be a rhododendron at all, she pushed her way into its branches. She crept along the wall behind the bush until she found a space large enough to curl up in. She pushed her shoes together and wadded up her stockings for a pillow. I'll never sleep, she thought as she lay down.

But she did. And her very last thought before she dropped off was of the magpie: Thieving scoundrel! She hoped its conscience — if it even had one — would keep it awake all night long.

chapter 13
THE BEE AND THE ROSE

Someone was singing a song Adela knew well. The singer's voice, tuneless and flat, was also well known to her. She smiled at the song's familiar refrain:

> *"The bee and the rose, the bee and the rose:*
> *Soft petals, sweet nectar are all the bee knows.*
> *And oh, my lady, my lady and me,*
> *My lady, the rose, and I, the bee."*

Adela stirred, rolled forward slightly, and smelled damp earth. Startled, she opened her eyes. For a moment, the green light around her was confusing.

Then she remembered where she was. She sat up and hit her head on a branch. "Ouch!"

The singing stopped abruptly. "Hello?"

"Garth?"

"Miss Adela? Where are you?"

She tried to see through the branches. "Are you alone?"

"I'm alone."

Adela crawled out of her hiding place, and Garth helped her to her feet. "What are you doing in there?" he asked.

She saw that he was still dressed in his finery from the day before, though everything looked a little worse for the wear. There was a stain on his jacket.

"I'm so glad you're all right!" she exclaimed. "Where's Marguerite?"

"Marguerite?" Garth looked puzzled.

"Marguerite! And the other guests! What happened last night? Did everyone go inside?"

"Oh, right! Last night! You should have been there, Miss Adela!"

"The front door was locked."

"Too bad for you! I had the best time of my life!"

Adela frowned.

Garth continued. "Here I was so worried about not getting along in fine society, but it wasn't like that at all. She's so wonderful, Miss Adela. I sat beside her during supper. She even let me hold her hand!"

So she had been right about Garth and Marguerite. They had forgotten about her! Adela put her hand to her head; it was aching. "Was there food?" she asked.

"Food? Well, I guess maybe there was—ham and beef and pies and cakes and such . . ." Garth laughed again. "Would you believe I was having such a good time I barely noticed?"

"I haven't eaten since our picnic yesterday."

"You should have come to the party."

"Well, I—I was worried." Adela was too embarrassed to explain why. "I'm glad Marguerite is all right," she said.

"Who?"

"Marguerite. When I couldn't find her yesterday, I worried something had happened to her." Adela forced out a small laugh. "I nearly convinced myself she'd been turned into—"

"Marguerite . . ." Garth interrupted, scratching his head. "Oh, *her*!"

"What do you mean . . . *her*? You said you sat with Marguerite at supper."

"No, I didn't! I sat with Lady Hortensia."

"But what about Marguerite?"

Garth shrugged. "How should I know?"

"Wasn't she with you at the party?"

"No. I was with Lady Hortensia. I held her hand."

To Adela's surprise, she saw that Garth was blushing. He ducked his head, then looked up. "I guess I can tell you, Miss Adela. I — I'm in love with her!"

"With Marguerite," Adela clarified.

"No, Miss Adela!" Garth sounded shocked. "It's Lady Hortensia I love!"

"But you must have seen Marguerite!"

Garth shook his head. "I don't think so."

"If she wasn't with you, then" — Adela felt as if her legs had turned to sand — "that means she's missing!"

"Is she, then?" said Garth without sounding as if he cared one way or the other.

"Oh, Garth! This is going to sound ridiculous, but I — I saw something yesterday. At least I think I saw something. It was Lady Hortensia, and —"

"Lady Hortensia!" Garth interrupted. "Oh, Miss

Adela, did I tell you about her? How she let me hold her hand at supper?"

"Marguerite was in the garden with her," Adela continued. "I was there; they didn't see me. And Hortensia — well, she did something to Marguerite. She . . ." How, Adela wondered, could this *not* sound ridiculous? "Well, I thought I saw her turn Marguerite into a daisy!"

She waited for Garth's reaction.

Which was a grin. "She's wonderful, isn't she?" said Garth.

"What?"

"Lady Hortensia! She's so beautiful and kind and —"

"Did you hear what I said?"

"What?"

"I said that I think I saw Hortensia change Marguerite into a daisy — using *magic* or . . . or something like that."

Garth chuckled. "You must've been imagining things, Miss Adela."

"Maybe," she agreed. "At least I hope I was. Only, I saw other things, too. There was a magpie, and it talked to me."

Garth's chuckle erupted into full laughter. "A talking magpie!"

"Well, I know it sounds idiotic! But I can't help but wonder if . . . Garth, what if Hortensia is some kind of witch?"

"A witch!"

"I might have imagined what I saw — maybe I'm going crazy — but what if I'm not?"

Garth shook his head. "Lady Hortensia is not a witch, Miss Adela. She's kind and beautiful and . . ." He paused, as if searching for the perfect word. "Did I tell you that she let me hold her hand?"

Only about a hundred times, thought Adela.

"She put her hand on my elbow, and I thought I would die, Miss Adela, right then and there. Then I got to lead her into the banquet hall, and I got to sit next to her the whole time. She let me hold her hand all through supper!"

For a moment, Garth looked blissful. Then his face fell, and he gave a groan.

"What is it?" asked Adela. Was Garth remembering something Hortensia had done? Something not right? Something . . . magic?

"The thing is—I don't know if she loves me! She wants me to be her gardener. That's good, isn't it?"

She felt like shaking the sense back into him. Instead, she said, "Her gardener?"

Garth pointed down the path, and Adela saw a painted white wheelbarrow. It looked more picturesque than practical, but it was filled with tools. "There's a rake and a shovel and a hoe—even a pruning saw!" said Garth. "She wouldn't ask me to be her gardener if she didn't care for me. Right?"

"You're already a gardener for the king," said Adela.

"I love her so much, Miss Adela. I'd do anything to make her happy."

She couldn't believe it: there were tears in Garth's eyes!

"Did I tell you she let me hold her hand?" he said.

A word came into Adela's mind then: *lovesick.* It was a word from the story she had thought of yesterday—the one about King Ival and the beautiful witch. The witch had enchanted Ival, turning him into a lovesick fool.

"I will love Lady Hortensia until the day I die!" Garth declared, and with a prickling of dread, Adela thought of another word from the same story: *bewitched.*

chapter 14
NEDDY

On the day after the party, Krazo was up with the sun, eager to arrange his new treasures. In his mind's eye, he could see exactly what he wanted: the coral-bead necklace coiled up at the bottom of his nest like a carpet, the diamond earrings and the necklace with the blue stone dangling from the domed ceiling like chandeliers, the emerald brooch, the turquoise-and-silver bracelet, the pearl ring, and the belt buckle propped up around the edges like paintings on a wall.

And yet, after working for more than an hour, after pushing this trinket here, that one there, Krazo found himself growing frustrated. Somehow, try as he might, he wasn't any closer to achieving his vision than when he had started. He stood in the middle of his nest and contemplated the problem.

Was it that his nest was too crowded? There were so many treasures now that Krazo couldn't turn around without bumping into one of them. But he didn't mind that. In fact, he liked being surrounded by so much wealth.

The problem, Krazo realized at last, was that he simply could not see his treasures — at least not well enough to appreciate them. The domed roof of sticks and twigs that arched over his nest was keeping out the light.

Why, he wondered, had this never bothered him before? Probably, he decided, because he had never been so rich before. Until today, when he had wanted to admire one of his treasures, he had dragged it into the light from an entrance. But now there were simply too many treasures for this to be practical.

The solution to the problem was obvious: he must remove the roof from his nest. In fact, when Krazo thought about it, he really had no need for a roof. It was designed to keep out rain and wind and predators. But it never rained on top of Flower Mountain; Hortensia's magic garden didn't *need* rain. Nor were there ever more than the gentlest of breezes here. As for predators, Krazo had never seen a single one. Yes, he decided, he must remove the roof.

Strangely, however, he made no move to do so. Instead he sat there in the dim light, clutching the coral beads with his claws. His mind was telling him something that he could not ignore.

All magpies have roofs over their nests, said his mind.

"Other birds have got nests without roofs," Krazo muttered in response.

But they aren't magpies, his mind argued.

"I want to see my treasures," Krazo insisted.

You're a magpie!

"I'm not!" Krazo croaked.

This absurd pronouncement shocked him, and the argument he was having with himself came to a halt, leaving Krazo free to follow a line of thinking he had never followed before. Was he not, he wondered, somehow different from other magpies?

Occasionally in his travels away from Hortensia's mountain, he had come across others of his kind — bold, black-and-white birds, almost always a group of them together. *Hello*, he would say. Depending on their mood, they would squawk back *Hello!* or *Go away!* If they seemed friendly, Krazo would try to start a conversation. He might ask if they knew of a good place to get food. Or, because he was usually on a scouting expedition for Hortensia, he might ask if they had ever heard of such-and-such a girl, and was she as pretty as was rumored? It didn't matter what he said. *Hello,* the other magpies would say, or *Go away,* as if they were incapable of saying anything else.

I'm not like them, Krazo realized.

But surely that didn't mean he wasn't one of them. He had the same plumage, the same long tail, the same black beak. He could understand their language, limited though it was. And this nest he had built — wasn't it just like theirs? Wasn't it a true magpie nest?

A nest that was too dark. Darker even than that room with the woman in it.

Krazo shuddered, ruffling his feathers. He had dreamed about the woman last night. "Oh, Neddy! Neddy, what are we to do?" she had cried, looking right at him, and Krazo had woken with a start, his heart pounding.

Who was Neddy, and what did Neddy have to do with him?

Krazo shook his head. He didn't want to think about the woman. He looked around his nest again. If I pull off the roof, he told himself, it will be light in here. I'll be able to see.

And so he started in. He tugged at the diamond earrings and the necklace with the blue stone, loosening them from the underside of the roof. After laying them carefully on the floor, he began pulling at the twigs above the entrance on the east side of his nest. First one, then another — Krazo pushed the twigs out of the nest. He yanked at a large twig, and a chunk of roof caved in on his head. He shook himself free of debris, pulled the belt buckle aside, moved the pearl earring to a safer location, and set to work in earnest. *Yank! Crash!* Out went chunks of roof. Krazo hopped from side to side, yanking and tossing. In his enthusiasm, he nearly threw the emerald brooch out with the rubbish. He snatched it back just in time and dropped it onto his pile of treasure.

Oh, what a difference it made to let the sunshine in! *Stop crying,* he felt like telling the woman in his dream. *Stop crying! We're rich!*

chapter 15
STRANGE SERVANTS

Was Garth under a magic spell? He certainly acted like it. Adela told him again what she had seen (or thought she had seen), and she showed him the daisy that might (or might not) be Marguerite. "You don't say," Garth commented, and went right back to the subject of Hortensia — how kind and beautiful she was, and how she had let him hold her hand — until Adela was tempted to hit him on the head with the shovel in his wheelbarrow. It was only after he had toddled off, humming "The Bee and the Rose," that it occurred to her that he might actually use his new tools. What if he felt inclined to prune something? Or rather, some*one*. She was about to run after him when she heard a sound coming from the other direction. Just in time, she dove behind a forsythia. She couldn't see who was coming, but she could hear footsteps. And then, "Good morning, my pretty little daisy!" said Hortensia. She continued along without stopping or looking back.

Adela peeked out from her hiding place. Hortensia was beautiful even from behind! Her dark hair hung loose down the back of her white lace gown. She was slender and graceful. How could anyone so lovely be a wicked witch? And what was that she was carrying under her arm? It looked like a portable writing desk. Cecile had one made of lacquered wood; it had a compartment under a hinged lid for storing paper and pen and a bottle of ink. Was Hortensia planning on writing? Was that something witches did?

Once again, Adela was filled with doubts. "Never mind," she told herself. "Hortensia's gone off to write something. While she's busy, I can find out the truth. I know I heard lots of people inside last night. The other guests might have been there. Marguerite might have been there, too, even if Garth didn't notice her." She was murmuring to herself, just like the cook at home, who was always cheering herself on as she worked: *Just a bit more flour then, and we'll have a nice pastry.* Thinking of the cook made Adela think of food. Garth had spoken of a supper. She was more than hungry; maybe she could find something to eat inside Hortensia's house.

To her relief, the front door was unlocked this morning. She slipped inside, closed the door behind her, and looked around. She was standing in an entrance hall with a white marble floor, walls papered in green and gold, and a curved staircase leading to a second floor. A huge window at the top of the stairs let in the morning sun. It all seemed normal enough — even welcoming.

There were several sets of double doors on either side of the entrance hall, all of them carved with elaborate floral designs. Adela peeked through one set and saw a large sitting room with two men standing at the far end of it. Their backs were toward her, and they were whisking feather dusters over the frame of an enormous, life-size portrait of Hortensia. Servants, Adela decided. But she couldn't make up her mind if their presence was comforting or not. Did witches have servants?

One of the men was elegantly dressed: his brocade coat, velvet breeches, silk stockings, and high-heeled shoes looked fancier than the footmen's uniforms at home. The other servant's clothes looked a trifle dowdy by comparison. In fact, they looked rumpled, as if he had been wearing them for some time. Adela waited for the men to turn around, but their feather dusters swished back and forth, back and forth across the base of the frame. The men weren't even looking at what they were doing; they were staring up at Hortensia, who gazed down at them with her lovely smile. A smile that might (or might not) belong to a witch.

It was the portrait, as lifelike as it was life-size, that helped Adela decide against making her presence known to the men. She tiptoed across the entrance hall to another a set of doors. Nudging them open, she saw a drawing room with tall windows and yet another portrait of Hortensia. The room was untidy, with pillows fallen off couches, chairs turned over, and playing cards tossed on and around several small gaming tables. There were dirty glasses and half-empty bottles lying about. Adela was just thinking that the portrait dusters would do better to spend their time in here when she saw that there was already a servant in the room. A young man lay stretched out in the middle of the parquet floor with his eyes closed, his hands laced behind his head, his ankles crossed, and a smile on his face. That he was a servant was apparent from the mop handle lying across his chest and the bucket of soapy water next to him. And yet he didn't exactly have the look of a working man. He was handsome, with long auburn curls and a beautifully trimmed, perfectly symmetrical mustache with curled tips. His clothes were adorned with an abundance of lace and embroidery, and they looked at least twenty or thirty years out of fashion. Indeed, the clothes looked as if they might actually be that old, for the lace was torn and the embroidery faded and coming out in places. Adela had just realized that one of the man's shoes was missing its heel when he stirred and moaned a few words that sounded vaguely like *Oh, my love!* He rolled over onto his side and began to snore.

Adela slipped into the drawing room, softly closed the door behind her, and tiptoed across the floor to another set of doors.

At last! Here was Hortensia's banquet hall! Here was the supper Garth had talked about — or, rather, the remains of it. Adela's empty stomach tightened at the sight of roasts with meat still hanging from the bones, half-eaten loaves of bread, plates of cheese and fruit, trays of cakes and tarts laid out on a long table covered with a white cloth. She seized a loaf of bread, tore off a piece, and stuffed it in her mouth. She bit into an apple, and the taste of its juice made her thirsty. She grabbed a glass pitcher full of water and drank her fill. She was just reaching for what looked like a cherry tart when she heard voices. By now, hiding when she didn't know what was coming had become instinctive: Adela grabbed the tart and ducked under the table.

A door in the corner of the room opened. Adela stuffed the tart into her mouth. She could see two pairs of feet (black leather shoes with gold buckles, red leather shoes with silver buckles) walking toward the table. Something clattered above her, and she could hear what sounded like dishes being loaded onto a tray.

"I get to wash," said a man's voice.

"You go right ahead," said another man. "Lady Hortensia said *I* was to dry. She told me she thinks drying is far more important than washing."

There was a brief silence. Even from under the table, Adela could tell it was a stony one. And then, "I don't believe you! She never said any such thing!"

exclaimed the first man. By now, Adela had figured out that he was the one with the black shoes.

"She did!" said the man with the red shoes. "She said if I dried the dishes and polished the silver, I could sit beside her at supper tonight."

"That's not fair!"

"She said I could hold her hand!" The man with the red shoes sounded smug.

"But *I* want to polish the silver! *I* want to hold her hand!"

"Sorry!" The man with red shoes didn't sound the least bit apologetic. "But it does seem as if it's *me* she loves."

There was a choked sound. Adela made a face. It sounded like the man with the black shoes was crying! And now the man with the red shoes was sniggering! They're being as ridiculous as Garth, she thought.

As ridiculous as Garth . . . Adela recalled the portrait dusters, staring up at Hortensia as they cleaned the same spot over and over. She recalled the young man asleep in the drawing room, moaning *Oh, my love!* And now these two idiots . . .

Was it possible that Hortensia's servants were under the same spell as Garth?

The last bit of tart slid down her throat. She felt less hungry now. In fact, she felt rather sick to her stomach.

They *are* under a spell, thought Adela. They are, and this is real, and I'm not imagining any of it. Hortensia *is* a witch!

What, she wondered, do I do now?

chapter 16
THE PACKET OF LETTERS

Not long after the roof was off his nest, Krazo received a summons from Hortensia. "Come! I'm in the garden!" she called, using magic to reach his mind. Krazo found the intrusion unpleasant, like having an itch in his brain. The only way to get rid of the itch was to submit.

In the garden meant under the rose tree, and it was there that Krazo headed. But as he flew over the garden, he saw something that made him turn in a wide circle: the gardener from yesterday's party was pushing a wheelbarrow down one of the paths. Where had that come from? Krazo wondered, even as he saw a familiar shape poking out of the wheelbarrow. Shovel, he thought.

He would have dropped down for a closer look if Hortensia hadn't sent another needle-like zap of magic through his brain. He straightened his course, heading for the rose tree. He spiraled down to the ground beside Hortensia's couch and landed (not by accident) on the very spot where her treasure lay buried.

"You certainly took your time," said Hortensia.

Krazo looked up. "Good morning, my lady. You look lovely today." He had no idea whether she looked lovely or not, but he knew from long experience that it was best to flatter his mistress. He saw that she was wearing a triple strand of pearls this morning. They were whiter than her lace morning dress; they looked like teeth against her golden skin. Krazo also admired the carved ivory combs in her hair. In itself, ivory was not really flashy enough for him, but these combs were set with tiny rubies.

"I don't know that I've ever enjoyed a party as much as yesterday's," said Hortensia. She was holding her portable writing desk in her lap. On top of the desk, which was made of polished black wood inlaid with mother-of-pearl, were a swan-feather quill pen, a bottle of ink, a bit of felt for blotting, and the satin-covered box that held her pink stationery. She folded a piece of paper and put it in an envelope. "I must say that the young men who came are *gorgeous*. That young gardener, in particular, is about as handsome as they come! And the girls provided all the usual entertainment."

Hortensia always took relish in going over the highlights of her garden parties, and it was Krazo's duty to listen and respond to her clever comments. "Did you *see* that plump shepherdess wearing bright orange?" his mistress would say. "Her gown practically screamed tulip at me." Then she would laugh heartily as she added, "Actually, *she* was the one who screamed when I turned her into one." Krazo would then respond with a *Keck-keck-keck-keck-keck*, which was his approximation of laughter. Not that he ever understood what was funny about the whole business, and he really didn't care much whether she changed a girl into a tulip, a trillium, or a trumpet vine.

"That little dairymaid told me all about her cows," Hortensia continued now. "Do you know that she actually *milks* them? The poor dear's hands were all red and calloused, though I will admit that the rest of her was quite pretty in a country sort of way. She made a sweet little primrose."

Krazo's mind began to wander. He thought of the shovel, of digging a hole, of finding treasure at the bottom of it.

"And I must say those twins were most diverting," Hortensia continued. "A little on the pale side, though I suppose the fact that there were two of them made up for that. Did you ever see so many freckles? Twice the usual amount, eh?"

Krazo was so preoccupied with thoughts of treasure that he nearly forgot to join in her laughter—*Keck-keck-keck-keck-keck.*

"As for that shopgirl, you'll find a new torch lily beside that big blue hydrangea—you know the hydrangea I mean—that one that used to be a seamstress. I caught the girl standing right beside it, flirting with Anthony and Paul."

Anthony and Paul, Krazo knew, had been at yesterday's party. Anthony was the son of a wealthy noble, and Paul was the son of a well-to-do miller. No doubt they were somewhere inside the house this morning. Hortensia's *conquests*—that was the word she used for the men who admired her—generally ended up there.

"I'm afraid the darling boys lost all interest in Torch Lily when I arrived," Hortensia went on. "I sent them on their way, and I could tell she was a bit piqued about it. She ought to try to hide that better, as it does nothing for her looks. Not that she has to worry about those any longer. Her flirting days are over. As are those of that daisy creature."

Daisy creature — that must be the girl with the diamonds. Thinking of her made Krazo remember the princess. Last night, when he wasn't having nightmares about the woman in the dark room, he had dreamed about the princess. She had cried again in his dream, but this time, when she had seen him, she had smiled and spoken in the same soothing voice she had used with the dairymaid. He liked that voice.

Just then Hortensia tossed him a packet of envelopes tied together with a white ribbon. "I've finished my letters," she said.

These letters were not invitations but carefully worded missiles addressed to the families of her guests. Krazo knew what they said because Hortensia often read them aloud as she wrote them, snickering when she reached the last few lines:

Dearest _____,

I write to tell you that I have asked your charming
daughter [or granddaughter or niece or ward, as
appropriate] to live with me and to deliver, with the
most profound pleasure, the news that _____ has
accepted my invitation. I cannot tell you how delighted
I am that she has consented to grace my happy home
with her lovely presence. You will be pleased to learn
that henceforth, _____ will be admired by all who
visit me. Indeed, I feel as if a beautiful flower has
been added to my garden. I thank you for so graciously
allowing me to transplant _____ to my home.

> *Hortensia*

A variation on this letter was the phrase *beautiful*
flower, for here Hortensia would occasionally name
the actual flower, in which case she would not only
snicker but also howl with laughter as she signed her
name.

There was a similar version of the letter for families
of her male guests, only that version didn't mention
the garden, and it was always phrased to suggest that

the young man had begged Hortensia to be allowed to stay on as a courtier.

Like her party invitations, these letters were written on magically scented paper. The magic must have been extremely powerful, because after one whiff, the recipients would swoon with joy and brag to their friends and neighbors: "Yes, that's right. Our little Mary's living with Lady Hortensia now! You have heard of Lady Hortensia, haven't you? They say she's got the most beautiful garden in the world." Krazo, whose job it was to deliver the letters, had seen it happen often enough. The magic grew stronger over time, until, at last, everyone who had ever known one of Hortensia's guests — even family members — forgot about them.

For those guests who had come to the party by coach, it was Hortensia's practice to send the letters home with the coachmen, whom she cleverly enchanted so that they would remember nothing untoward about their brief visit to Flower Mountain. Krazo knew Hortensia must have sent the coachmen from yesterday's party home already. It would be his job to deliver the remaining letters today.

"What about the princess?" he asked.

He couldn't have said why it mattered to him, but

he did want to know what had happened to her. What flower had she become? Where was she in the garden?

But Hortensia sat up, a look of alarm on her face. "The princess? I forgot about her!"

Krazo tilted his head. In his experience, Hortensia had never forgotten about a guest before.

"Are you sure she came? Did you see her?" asked Hortensia.

Much as he wanted to lie, Krazo knew it could be dangerous. "Yes."

"When? Where?"

"Yesterday . . . in the garden."

Hortensia groaned. "How could I have been so careless?"

"Maybe she went home with the coachman," Krazo suggested.

"She couldn't have! I know she wasn't in the carriage! And the gate was locked at all other times. She must be on the grounds somewhere." Hortensia picked up the pen and dipped it in the ink bottle. "The coachman may have reached home by now. They'll be wondering what's happened to her."

She whipped out a piece of stationery. She didn't laugh as she wrote the letter; instead she snarled,

"Flower, indeed! I'll wager the girl's as ugly as a clump of sod. I don't know what I'll do with her, but I can assure you that it won't be pretty!" She addressed an envelope, shoved the new letter inside, and added it to Krazo's bundle.

"Make sure you deliver the king's letter first," she told him. "Go! Now, as fast as you can! I'll rip your tail feathers out if there's any trouble over this."

Krazo would never have dared point out that it was hardly his fault she had forgotten the princess. But he did think it as he looped the ribbon around his neck.

The packet was heavy, and at first he wobbled in his flight. He had to circle the garden several times before he found his balance. He saw Hortensia gather up her writing things and leave her marble couch. He saw her intercept the gardener on a nearby path. The gardener took the writing desk from her, and the two of them hurried toward the house.

And then, because the thought of tail feathers being pulled out was not a pleasant one, Krazo hurried on his way.

chapter 17
DANGEROUS

It wasn't long before the argument in the banquet hall attracted attention. The servant who had been sleeping in the next room came in first; Adela, still trapped under the table, recognized him by his missing heel. This servant began arguing that mopping the floor was more important than doing the dishes. Then came the two feather dusters, insisting that Hortensia considered their work superior to any other. Soon more servants showed up, until the banquet hall was filled with men squabbling over whose job was most essential and who would get to sit next to Hortensia at supper that evening. Adela was just wondering if she should try sneaking out the door when a new voice, loud enough to be heard over the rest, called out, "Gentlemen, enough!"

The words "My lady!" buzzed around the room. Adela, looking toward the door, saw the hem of a white gown.

Hortensia waited for quiet. And then, "I regret to inform you that we have a problem. There is a young girl who came to the party yesterday. Her name is *Adela*," she said, making the name sound distasteful.

"Do you mean Princess Adela? I saw her yesterday," said someone. Adela thought she recognized the voice as belonging to one of the guests she had met the day before.

"You're sure? A rather plain girl? Rather *ugly*?" said Hortensia.

"Well, I—"

Another voice broke in: "I saw her this morning in the garden. I talked to her."

It was Garth! Adela bit her lip.

"She was acting strange," said Garth. "Something about daisies and magic and—"

Hortensia cut him off. "Where did she go?"

"I don't know, my lady!"

"Listen to me, all of you! This girl—this princess—is dangerous."

"Miss Adela—dangerous?" Garth sounded incredulous. "Are you sure, my lady?"

"Of course I'm sure. You'll understand how frightened I am when I tell you that the girl has gone completely mad!"

"Mad!"

"An unfortunate condition caused by a combination of mountain air and too much sun. It's hard to say what horrible things she might do. I'm afraid for my life!"

"I can't believe Miss Adela would hurt anybody."

"Then you're a fool!" Hortensia snarled. She stamped her foot, but when she spoke again, her voice was honeyed and sorrowful. "Or, more likely, you don't care about me."

"No, my lady! Why, I would die to protect you!"

The other men rumbled in agreement.

Hortensia clapped her hands and raised her voice. "The man who loves me the most will be the one who finds the princess and brings her to me. That man will sit beside me at supper tonight."

The rumbling of the men was louder this time.

"Do you want her alive or dead, my lady?" asked Garth.

Adela was hard put to decide which was worse — the question or Hortensia's quick answer: "Alive, naturally! Alive if at all possible! I have never had a *garden princess* before. Go on, now — quickly! Search the garden! Search the grounds!"

There was a scuffle as the men fought to get out the door. Only Garth lingered behind with Hortensia. "I don't want to leave you alone, my lady," he said. "If anything happened to you, I couldn't live with myself. I would have brought Miss Adela to you this morning if I'd only known."

"We'll find her soon enough. The front gate is locked, and she can't get out. She may even be inside the house."

"I know where she'll be, my lady. Miss Adela loves flowers. I'd guess that she still does, even if she has gone mad. She'll be in the garden."

"Very well, then. Show me!"

Adela saw Hortensia's skirt swirl around. She peeked out from under the tablecloth just in time to see her leave the room, Garth hurrying behind. She listened to their retreating footsteps. She heard the far-off noise of the front door opening and closing.

The house was quiet.

Adela let out her breath. *Dangerous,* Hortensia had called her. But how dangerous could she be, crouched under a table with no way of defending herself?

She listened to the faint voices of the men outside. "Oh, Princess! Where are you?" And "Come out, come out, wherever you are!" Just as if it were a game of hide-and-seek! It was only a matter of time before they came to look for her inside the house. She had to do something — find a better place to hide. If only she could stay hidden until . . .

Until what? Until someone came to rescue her? By now her father and Cecile must be wondering where she was. But they would have no reason to suspect any mischief. If anything, they would assume that the partygoers had had a late start coming back and had decided to spend the night at Hortensia's or at some inn along the way.

And when she and Marguerite didn't come home today? Cecile would surely begin to fret, but Adela's father had never been one for worrying. "I expect the carriage has broken down," he would say. "I'll send someone to look for them." And what good would whoever he sent be against a witch who could turn girls into flowers and men into witless slaves?

I can't just sit here waiting, thought Adela. I have to rescue myself.

The front gate was locked, yes, but there must be a key for it somewhere. The keys at home were kept near the servants' entrance, just off the kitchen. Keys for all the doors in the palace, keys for the stables, keys for the various outhouses, keys for all the gates — all hanging from hooks neatly labeled by the housekeeper. Was it too much to hope for something like that here?

Apparently it was. Adela found the kitchen quickly enough, but there were no keys to be found there — only stacks of dirty dishes. "Never mind! There are other places," she told herself.

She began to look in earnest, slipping from room to room, opening drawers and cupboards, lifting the lids of chests, and peeking inside boxes. She was careful to stay away from the windows. Even so, she felt as if she were being watched by all the images of Hortensia. They were everywhere: portraits on walls, miniature pictures set out on tables, busts on pedestals. At least she has one weakness, thought Adela. She must be as vain as anything.

Unfortunately, Adela couldn't think how to use Hortensia's weakness to any advantage. She found herself wondering what King Ival would have done. How, for example, had he escaped from the beautiful witch who had enchanted him? Adela couldn't remember. But she did recall another story in which King Ival had come up against a witch so ugly that she went about cloaked in a dense fog. In that one, he had been helped out by a friendly mole who could see in the dark. And there was also the story illustrated by the tapestry in the library back home. In that one, King Ival had been helped by a dog who had turned out to be an enchanted princess. Helpful animals under enchantments were a common theme in stories about King Ival.

Adela couldn't help thinking of the magpie. "Enchanted prince?" she wondered aloud.

Hardly. Enchanted thief was more like it! She couldn't imagine any creature less interested in helping her. She was just going to have to help herself.

Upstairs she found a long, carpeted hallway lined with doors and, naturally, more portraits. Pushing open one door, she found a room with four unmade beds, a wardrobe, a dresser, and yet another portrait of Hortensia. She opened the wardrobe; it was empty. She pulled open the dresser drawers, and they were empty as well. Not even a stocking, thought Adela.

The next few rooms were the same: unmade beds, empty wardrobes, and empty dressers. So it was with all the rooms, until there was only one door left, only one more room to search, and Adela despaired of ever finding the key.

But her hopes lifted when she opened this door.

Unlike the other rooms, this one was filled with clothes. There were dresses everywhere — crammed into the wardrobe, tossed over the chairs, and lying in heaps on the floor. It's her room, thought Adela. If there is a key, this is where I'll find it.

The dressing table looked promising. What a mess it was! Piles of jewelry — bracelets and brooches, earrings and necklaces, tossed together as if they were junk. Adela lifted a golden belt. It was heavy enough to be real gold; the gemstones studding its length looked real, too. And here was the very diamond necklace Marguerite had worn yesterday. Adela picked it up, feeling the weight of the stones in her hand. She wondered if everything on the dressing table was stolen. Was that why Hortensia held her garden parties? So she could add to her jewelry collection? If so, she had been at it a long time. Adela thought of all the flowers in the garden — hundreds of them. How could it be that nobody knew what Hortensia was doing? "Somebody needs to stop her," she murmured.

She had been talking to herself all day; now, however, she had someone to talk *to* — her own reflection, looking back at her from the mirror above the dressing table. But there was something strange about the reflection. Adela stared, putting her hand up to her hair. The girl in the mirror did the same. But where Adela's hand touched the tangled remains of Marguerite's careful hairdressing, the hand in the mirror touched a beautiful arrangement of curls. Adela looked down at her dress. Not only was it torn, but it was also filthy. Which was what happened when you wore a dress that was too small and tried to sleep in it on the ground. She looked up again to confirm that the girl in the mirror was wearing the same blue dress. Except that the dress in the mirror was clean and fresh. Not only that, but the gown also fit perfectly; nobody could ever say the girl in the mirror was too large for it. In fact, it seemed to Adela that the girl in the mirror was rather slender. She leaned forward, wondering if the girl's face wasn't different as well. Her lips seemed more full, her eyebrows more arched, her eyelashes longer, her nose straighter . . . In a word, the girl in the mirror was beautiful.

Adela set the diamond necklace down and picked up an enameled bracelet. So did the girl in the mirror. Adela dropped the bracelet. So did the girl. "I suppose it's a magic mirror," said Adela. "It makes you look more beautiful than you really are. But I can't see why Hortensia needs a mirror like that."

She turned her head, trying to see her profile. "Try not to frown, dear," Cecile was always telling her. "You have a rather weak chin, and frowning doesn't suit you, especially in profile." Now Adela frowned, and it seemed to her that her reflection looked quite pretty. She tried smiling and found that her reflection was dazzling. Then she remembered how Marguerite had looked at Garth — sideways, shy yet flirtatious, her head slightly lowered so she could show off her eyelashes. Adela tried looking at herself like that, smiling as if she had a secret to share, and her reflection was so lovely that she could have admired it forever.

Instead she closed her eyes and shook her head. "What am I doing?" she wondered aloud.

She opened her eyes. The girl in the mirror was still as pretty as ever. "I've got to get out of here," Adela told her. Naturally, the girl in the mirror said the same thing, but she said it so beautifully that Adela found herself staring at her again.

"Stop it," Adela admonished herself.

She averted her eyes, and it was in doing so that she saw it — exactly what she needed to see and exactly when she needed to see it: a silver key on a silver chain, hanging over a corner of the frame of the mirror. It felt like magic, finding it like that.

She took the key down. It wasn't very large. The palace gates at home had a big iron key. You needed two hands to turn it. But this little key was the only one Adela had found. "It must be the right one!" she said.

The girl in the mirror looked as if she agreed. Her beautiful eyes sparkled with excitement, and for a moment, Adela felt as if the girl were on her side, as if she wanted her to escape, to stop Hortensia. It was as if the girl were saying, *You were meant to find that key. You were meant to be a hero.* And then the temptation to stare came over Adela again. She could do nothing but gaze at the loveliness of the girl in the mirror. Everyone who looked at that girl would love her. How could they not?

Adela frowned. So did the girl in the mirror, looking even more fetching.

"You're not me," said Adela. The girl in the mirror said the same thing, only she looked sad as she said it.

And, of course, beautiful.

"I have to go," said Adela. She reached out with her calloused, sunburned hand as if to touch the porcelain white hand of the girl on the other side of the glass. Then she turned away.

Just outside the window on the other side of the room was an oak tree. Adela opened the window, hitched up her skirt, and pulled herself up onto the sill. The tree grew so close to the house that she had no trouble swinging over to the nearest bough. She reached back to close the window, then climbed into a sanctuary of shadowy green. She could hear the searchers calling for her — "Come on out, Princess! We won't hurt you!" — but she couldn't see them, and that was all to the good. "If I can't see them, they can't see me," she told herself as she settled into a fork of the tree. She would wait until dark to make her escape. And then . . .

Adela's hand closed around the silver key. "I'll tell Father what's happened," she murmured, "and we'll put an end to it."

How she or her father would do that, she had no idea. But that was how she felt. As if she were destined not only to escape from Hortensia but to defeat her as well. As if she were exactly what Hortensia had called her. Not ugly. Not mad. But *dangerous*.

chapter 18
THE RETURN OF KRAZO

It was late when Krazo returned from delivering Hortensia's letters. He expected to find the usual party going on inside the house: music and laughter pouring out of windows opened to the night air. Instead, he had a surprise.

The windows were open, but Krazo couldn't hear any music. And when he landed on the sill of a window outside the banquet hall, he saw that the men seated around the table looked gloomy rather than merry. They were picking at their food, casting nervous glances at one another and at Hortensia, who sat alone at the head of the table, looking sour and silent.

When one of the men reached for a pitcher as if to fill her wineglass, she glowered at him.

What was going on? Did it have something to do with the princess? Krazo had been thinking about her all day, wondering if Hortensia had found her yet, hoping that she hadn't. An impossible hope! Now he wondered if the princess had cried when Hortensia had found her, and for some reason, a catch came into his throat. He shook his head as if to rid himself of even the thought of her crying. He turned from the window and was about to take off for his nest when he saw someone move on the far side of the lawn. A girl was standing at the front gate.

Heart pounding, he launched himself into the air. He flew across the lawn and landed on the grass behind the princess.

She whirled around. "You!" She glared at him and turned away. Her hands were fumbling with the lock on the gate. "Go away!" she said over her shoulder.

There was not much to like in her voice at the moment, but Krazo hardly cared. Just to see her, when he had thought he would never see her again, made him feel as if he had been borne up by a draft of air. "What are you doing?" he asked.

"None of your business! Leave me alone!"

Was she angry? Krazo had seen Hortensia get angry before — all teeth and snarls, like a wolf. But there were no teeth, no snarls, no wolf inside the princess.

He hopped closer, trying to see what she was doing. She had something in her hand — something made of silver. She was trying to turn the silver thing in the lock, but it wouldn't turn.

"It's no good!" said the princess. She moaned, laying her head against the gate, and it occurred to Krazo that she might cry again.

He was of half a mind to retreat to a safe distance, but the silver thing, now dangling from her fingers, caught his attention. He stared at it, then hopped closer, unable to believe his eyes. "Where did you get that?"

The princess lifted her head.

He stretched his neck toward the key. "Where did you get it?" he asked.

"It's only a key. I found it in the house. I thought it might open the gate."

Not a gate but a box, thought Krazo. A silver box with treasure inside.

"I should have known it would be too small," said the princess. "I suppose *you* want it!"

He did. He wanted the treasure.

"You can have it," said the princess, dropping the key on the ground. "It's no good to me. She'll find me soon, and . . ." But she didn't finish her sentence, and Krazo saw that her eyes were filled with tears.

Don't cry, he thought.

The princess wiped her eyes, but more tears came to fill them up.

Krazo remembered his dream—the woman crying in the room. He knew that if he could only give the woman the treasure, she would stop crying. The treasure would fix everything. It would make her happy.

"Don't cry!" he begged the princess. And when she wiped her eyes again, he said, "Can you dig a hole?"

chapter 19

A REQUEST FOR HELP

Adela was certain she had misunderstood the magpie. "A hole? Why would I want to dig a hole?" she said.

"Treasure!"

"What treasure?"

"In the box."

"A box with treasure inside it?"

"In the ground." The magpie picked up the silver key with its foot, holding it toward her. "Locked," it said.

Was that what the key was for? A box of treasure, buried in the ground? Adela felt the tears coming again.

"Don't cry! We're rich!" said the magpie.

Which made her laugh. As laughter went, it was of the bitter sort, but it was better than crying. "I don't want to be rich," she told the magpie. "I want to get away."

She had been so sure the key would open the gate—as if she were the hero in a story, certain to triumph because she deserved to.

"There is a shovel," said the magpie. "There!"

Adela looked in the direction it wagged its head. Garth's wheelbarrow was sitting beside the fountain in front of the house. She had noticed it earlier; if she hadn't already known that Garth wasn't his usual self, the fact that he had left his tools outside all night would have been a clue that something wasn't right. "Yes, I see the shovel," she told the magpie. "Only, I don't suppose you can understand this, but Hortensia is looking for me. She's going to turn me into a petunia or something if I don't get away from here. I don't have time to help you dig for buried treasure." And I don't trust you, she thought.

"Please help," said the magpie.

Please help. Something about these words made Adela waver. They made her think of King Ival. The enchanted animals that helped him usually did so because he had helped them first. The magpie could very well be enchanted. If she helped it dig up some treasure, would it help her escape?

Don't be so gullible, Adela told herself. You're not King Ival. And this isn't a particularly helpful magpie. It's only being greedy. All the same, she couldn't help feeling curious. "How do you know there's buried treasure?" she asked.

"I saw it."

"Where? When?"

She listened as the magpie explained in its halting, croaking voice. Apparently it had seen Hortensia look inside a box. It had seen Hortensia lock the box with the very same key Adela had found, then bury the box in the garden in the middle of the night.

"But you didn't see what was in the box," said Adela.

"No," the magpie acknowledged.

"Then I don't understand how you know it's treasure."

"What else?"

"It could have been anything! Besides, if it were treasure, why should Hortensia keep it buried in the garden? Why not keep it with the rest of her things? I saw what was in her bedroom. What could be more valuable than that?"

"More treasure," said the magpie. "Better treasure."

Adela was skeptical. If Hortensia was as fond of treasure as she seemed — so fond that she orchestrated these garden parties in order to enchant her guests and steal their jewelry — would she really bury her best treasure? Wouldn't she want to display it?

But if the box didn't contain treasure, then what *had* she buried? What did she need to keep hidden? And from whom?

An idea was sizzling in Adela's mind like the fuse on a firework. The firework went off. "It's 'The Dog Princess'!" she exclaimed.

" 'Dog princess'?" asked the magpie.

"It's a story."

"What is a story?"

"It's something you read or tell . . ."

"Tell *me*!"

Adela shook her head. "Not here. Let's get the shovel. You can show me where the box is buried, and I'll tell you on the way."

chapter 20
THE DOG PRINCESS

As rickety as Garth's wheelbarrow was, Adela was pleased to find nothing wrong with his shovel. She took care to be silent as she worked it free from the other tools, casting a wary glance at the lighted windows above her. It would be the end of everything if anyone heard her.

She rested the shovel on her shoulder and followed the magpie as it hopped around the house. "Story?" said the bird when they reached the garden.

How do you tell a story to a magpie? she wondered, then decided on the ordinary way. "Once upon a time," she began, "there was a wicked sorcerer who lived in

the mountains and raised dragons. The dragons terror-
ized the people living in the valley below, and —"

"What is a sorcerer?" asked the magpie. "What are
dragons?"

"A sorcerer is someone who performs magic — like
Hortensia," said Adela. "And dragons are horrible
creatures. They eat sheep and cattle and —"

"Wolves eat sheep and cattle," said the magpie.

"Dragons are much worse than wolves. Hadn't
we better go? You need to show me where the box is
buried."

The magpie began to hop along the path, and Adela
followed, continuing the story as she walked: "The
people were so frightened of the dragon that they went
to King Ival for help."

The magpie came to a stop and looked up at her.
"King EYE-vull?"

"He's the hero," Adela explained.

"What is a hero?"

"A hero is . . . a very brave person. King Ival is
always the hero in stories."

"Why?"

"Because he just is!"

"Why?"

"Because there's always some villain that has to be defeated."

"What is a villain?"

They would never get anywhere at this rate! "A villain is someone very bad—like Hortensia," said Adela. "Please hurry!"

On they went, and she continued. "The sorcerer is the villain in this story. King Ival finds his hideout in the mountains, spies on him, and notices that he drinks out of a special flask every night."

"What is a flask?" said the magpie, stopping again. It seemed to be unable to ask questions and move forward at the same time.

"It's a kind of bottle," Adela explained impatiently. "The sorcerer keeps it in a cupboard that's guarded by a dragon with seven heads. That's how Ival knows the flask is important."

"How?"

"Because why would he have a dragon guarding the cupboard if it weren't? Anyway, Ival decides to steal the flask. So he does, and—"

"How does he steal it?"

"He kills the dragon! Look, this part doesn't matter all that much. Please keep going!"

The magpie hopped forward again, and Adela went on. "So, Ival's about to drink from the flask when the dog stops him."

The magpie stopped again. "What dog?"

Oh, no! Had she really forgotten to mention the dog? Adela let out a sigh. "What happened was that on his way to the find the sorcerer, Ival met up with a dog. He helped the dog; he took a thorn out of its paw, and after that, the dog followed him. So the dog was there when Ival stole the flask, and it jumped up and tried to stop him from drinking from it."

The magpie opened its beak as if to ask another question, but Adela rushed on with the story. "So Ival knocks the dog away and tries to drink from the flask again. This time the dog comes at him as if it's going to attack. Ival draws his sword, and he's just about to kill the dog when the sorcerer shows up. And you think it's all over for King Ival. But . . ." Adela paused for effect. The magpie leaned forward. "Just in time," she continued, "the dog picks up the flask in its mouth and tosses it into the fireplace. The flask breaks, and the liquid inside it explodes. The fire blazes up, and the sorcerer keels over dead."

She waited for the magpie's reaction.

There was none.

"The liquid in the flask was a magic potion that gave the sorcerer his power," said Adela. "When it exploded, he was destroyed."

Again, no reaction. Adela could see that she was going to have to explain the connection. "I think the box you saw is like the flask in the story. I think the box contains something magical that gives Hortensia her power, just as the flask contained the magic potion. Once we destroy it, Hortensia will be destroyed."

"What's in the box is treasure," said the magpie.

"We'll have to see, won't we?" Adela was disappointed by the bird's reaction. Disappointed and a little disheartened. Maybe her idea was a bit far-fetched. . . .

"What happened to the dog?" asked the magpie.

"The dog? Oh! Well, it turned out the dog was really a princess who had been put under a spell by the sorcerer. Once he was dead, the princess turned back into herself."

"Spell?" said the magpie.

"A *spell* is a kind of magic. Someone bad like a sorcerer or a witch—"

"A villain," said the magpie.

"Yes. A *villain* casts a spell on you and turns you into something you're not."

The magpie tilted its head. "Are you a dog?" it asked.

Adela couldn't help laughing. "No! And usually it's the other way around. It's a person who gets turned into something. For example, *you* might be under a spell. After all, magpies don't usually talk. You might be a princess —"

"Not a princess!"

"Or a prince."

The bird's feathers were puffed up, as if with indignation. "Not a prince! A magpie!" It took off down the path, and Adela had to run to keep up.

"Where are we going?" she called.

The answer came when the bird turned through an opening in a wall.

They were in the courtyard with the rose tree.

Adela stared. The tree seemed much larger than it had before, the scent of its roses even more powerful. She wondered if it was a person like every other flower in the garden.

"Dig here," said the magpie, scratching at the ground near the roots of the tree.

Adela waited for the magpie to move out of the way, then lifted the shovel and drove it into the soil.

A branch scraped against her neck. "Ow!" She reached up and felt wetness. "I'm bleeding!"

The tree's branches were swaying as if moved by a breeze. Had there been a breeze? "Did you see that?" she said. "I think the tree scratched me!"

"Hurry up!" said the magpie.

She pushed the shovel into the earth again.

"Ow!" Adela jumped away, and the shovel clattered to the ground. This time the tree had hit her on the head, and she was sure there had been no wind. "Is this an enchanted tree?" she asked the magpie. "Is it a person?"

"Not a person," said the magpie.

It's probably lying, thought Adela. The tree must be a person — and an angry one at that!

She picked up the shovel, this time shifting her position so she could keep her eye on the tree. Even so, she wasn't ready for what happened. As she raised her arms, a branch reached out and snatched the shovel away, hurling it at the far wall of the courtyard. Another branch grabbed Adela's arm and dug its thorns into her flesh. Still another wrapped itself around her waist, pinning her other arm to her side. She cried out, twisting her body, and the branches tightened their grasp. Adela managed to free one arm, the thorns tearing her skin, but the branch came whipping back.

"Get away! Get away!" screeched the magpie.

"I can't!"

Adela batted away one branch after another. She clawed at the branch around her waist, but it was no use. She was crying now — her tears were flowing as freely as her blood, but she hardly noticed. She tried to grab for something — anything — to save herself, and her fingers closed around a rose. She pulled and felt the petals fall apart. The branch around her waist loosened. Before it could tighten again, she threw out her arm and found another bloom. She wrenched it from the tree and felt the branch coming unwound. Unfortunately, the other branches were holding on as tight as ever, and more were on the attack. One hit her on the face. Adela knocked it away with her free hand. "Get the flowers!" she shouted.

The magpie zoomed in and out from the tree,

grabbing one bloom, then another, so that petals flew like drops of blood. Adela ripped away another bloom, felt the branches around her waist loosen, and wrenched herself free. A branch grabbed her leg, pulling her back. She threw herself forward, using her own weight to break free. Another branch grabbed her foot, but she kicked it aside. The branches whipped about, snatching at the magpie and then — when the bird retreated to a safe distance — at the air.

Adela groaned from pain. "I knew it! It *is* an enchanted tree! Tell me the truth. Did you ever see Hortensia turn someone into this tree?"

"No!" The magpie hopped toward her.

"Has it always been here?"

"No. Not until she buried the box."

"What?" Adela sat up.

"She made it come up out of the ground."

"Out of nothing?"

Adela studied the rose tree. She was certain it would attack again if she tried to dig. "It's another magic spell," she said, thinking aloud. "She put the tree here for protection, like the seven-headed dragon in the story."

"Protecting her treasure," said the magpie.

"Protecting what she doesn't want us to find," said Adela. "But we are going to find it. I am going to dig up that box if it's the last thing I do. I just need something to fight with. A sword, or — I know! A pruning saw! There's one in the wheelbarrow. Come on!"

chapter 21
LOVELY AND LOVED

It was too much to ask that the pruning saw be at the top of the jumbled mess in Garth's wheelbarrow. Adela saw immediately that she was going to have to hunt for it. "Quiet!" croaked the magpie as she started to move tools aside.

She didn't need the warning. She wished Garth had not left the wheelbarrow quite so close to the front of the house. The lights were still on inside, and although there was no music tonight, Adela was certain people were still awake. Suppose someone looked outside.

Then she spied the saw under a coil of rope. "It's perfect!" she whispered to the magpie. "I'll go for the branches with this while you attack the blooms—"

She was just lifting the coiled rope when she heard a sound. She whirled around and saw that the front door had been thrown open. A figure was silhouetted in the light. "Miss Adela?"

She began to run, heading around the house. If she could get to the garden, she might be able to hide. But she couldn't see in the dark. Her foot struck a tree root and she tumbled forward. A moment later, Garth was upon her.

"Miss Adela! It's me!" He tried to help her up.

"Let me go!"

He gripped her wrist.

"Stop! You're hurting me!"

He couldn't *not* hurt her. There wasn't an inch of her skin that wasn't covered with cuts.

"You're bleeding, Miss Adela! What's happened to you?"

"Please! Let me go!"

But he was leading her back to the front of the house, even as she struggled to escape. "There, now!" said Garth. "Don't be frightened." He pulled her to the fountain and set her down on the edge of it, gripping her wrist with one hand and using the other to find his handkerchief. He dipped it in the water and dabbed at her cheek. "You look as if you've had a fight with a cat!"

His voice was so kind that tears filled her eyes. "Only a rose tree," said Adela.

"Trying to do a bit of pruning, were you?"

"No!" Adela tried to pull away again, but Garth held tight. He rinsed the handkerchief in the water and resumed his ministrations.

Adela dropped her voice to a whisper. "Garth, please listen to me! Everything here is magic — even the plants are under a spell. *You're* under a spell —"

"There you go again, poor thing! Lady Hortensia says it's the mountain air —"

"Lady Hortensia is a witch! Why can't you believe me? I can show you. . . ."

If he came with her — if she could show him the rose tree — he would see for himself.

"You're wrong, Miss Adela," Garth said firmly. "Lady Hortensia is good. She only wants to help you. Come on inside and you'll see."

"No!" She jerked her arm free and jumped to her feet, but this time Garth grabbed her from behind, pinning her arms to her side. He pushed her toward the open front door.

"My lady!" Garth bellowed. "I've found her, my lady!" And then, "Stop struggling, Miss Adela! You'll only hurt yourself."

"Let me go!"

But it was too late.

Adela saw the figure of Hortensia in the doorway, and a sob escaped from her. She tried to pull away again, and Garth's grip tightened. "It's just as you said, my lady! She's not herself at all."

Adela shoved back against Garth with all her weight so that he had to let go or lose his balance. At last, she was free! She turned to run. She took one step and then, to her horror, she couldn't go farther. Something was wrong with her feet. They wouldn't move!

"You may go inside, my dear boy," said Hortensia, her voice calm.

Now it was not only Adela's feet but her entire body that would not move.

"Are you sure, my lady?"

"She won't hurt me."

"I *will* hurt her!" shouted Adela, even though that seemed highly improbable at the moment. What was wrong with her? Why couldn't she move? "Don't listen to her, Garth! She has you under a spell! She's going to put me under one, too! She's a witch, I tell you! She's—" But Adela choked on her words, her tongue suddenly as immobile as the rest of her.

Garth said, "You told us whoever found the princess would sit beside you, my lady! I found her!"

"Yes," said Hortensia as she walked toward them. "But you must go inside and wait for me there."

"You'll come soon?"

"Very soon." Hortensia brushed her hand against Garth's cheek.

He grinned and headed for the house. The door didn't even have time to close behind him before Adela heard him call out, "I've found her! I've found the princess, and my lady is going to sit beside me!"

Adela opened her mouth, struggling to speak. Hortensia made a small gesture with her hand, and Adela's voice returned. "Garth! Help!" she shouted.

Hortensia laughed. "He's not going to listen to you."

"What have you done to him? You've bewitched him, haven't you?"

"My dear girl, have you never seen a man in love before?"

"Garth doesn't love you!"

Hortensia raised her eyebrows. "If that isn't love, I don't know what is." Then, before Adela could answer, she put her hand to her mouth in mock surprise. "Oh, but don't tell me! You think he's in love with you!"

"I do not!" Adela protested.

"But, of course, you do! How could I have missed it?" Hortensia's voice oozed pity. It was horrible to be frozen, to have to stand still and listen to her. "Garth has spoken of your kindness toward him," said Hortensia. "That's what he calls it — did you know? *Kindness*. But you and I know that your feelings are more than simply kindness —"

"They are not!" said Adela.

Hortensia made a small noise that implied disbelief. "I'm sure Garth has been kind to you as well. He is a very friendly young man. I can understand how a girl like you might mistake friendship for something else."

It was the way she emphasized those words — *a girl like you* — that prompted Adela to say, "What are you talking about?" But even as she asked the question, a voice in her mind warned, Don't ask her! Don't listen to her!

"Only the fact that you are not what anyone would

call pretty." Hortensia paused, as if gauging Adela's reaction. "Has no one ever told you that before?"

Adela couldn't help but think of the many ways her stepmother had implied as much. "I don't care what I look like. I care about what I *do*."

"My dear girl, we all *do* things. But some of us look more beautiful as we do them! Now, really, I must stop, for I can see that I have hurt your feelings. Truly, it must be hard to love Garth and know that he cannot love you in return."

"I do *not* love Garth!"

"Well, if it isn't Garth, it will be someone else," said Hortensia. Then her tone brightened. "Though, really, I think you're quite lucky!"

"Lucky?" said Adela.

"Why, being a princess! It doesn't matter what you look like — you'll still have plenty of willing suitors."

Hortensia couldn't have come closer to echoing Adela's father if she had tried: *What does it matter how tall she is or what she looks like? . . . She's the king's daughter. Who isn't going to want to marry her?* At the memory of her father's words, Adela felt tears spring to her eyes.

"Oh, dear! I've said quite the wrong thing again, haven't I?" said Hortensia. "I suppose you're one of those girls who hope they'll find someone who cares about what's in your heart."

Adela swallowed.

"You like to believe that a man will love you for who you are. Isn't that right?"

"Stop it!" said Adela.

"Isn't that right?" Hortensia pressed.

"Yes! People *do* love each other for what's inside!" Adela felt as if the confession were being ripped from her.

"They love beauty," said Hortensia.

"They love other things! Like bravery and intelligence and kindness —"

"But they love beauty most of all," said Hortensia. "You saw that with your little friend Marguerite. Garth chose her, not you. And now he has chosen me."

"I never wanted Garth to choose me. And he *doesn't* love you! He loves Marguerite —"

"He thought she was pretty," Hortensia said dismissively. "A pretty little daisy."

"I *saw* what you did to her!" said Adela.

Hortensia shrugged. "I only gave Marguerite what she wanted."

"What she wanted!" sputtered Adela.

"To be looked at, to be loved."

"So you turned her into a flower?"

"What else? Can you truly say that you have never wanted to be looked at like that—to be loved like that?" asked Hortensia.

"No! I have not!"

"I don't believe you," said Hortensia. She gazed into Adela's eyes, and Adela could not look away. Hortensia gazed and gazed—for how long, it was hard to tell. Adela felt her mind grow dreamy and wistful, until it seemed as if she *did* want what Hortensia said she wanted—to be admired for her beauty, *loved* for her beauty. Adela thought of Hortensia's mirror—how lovely her reflection had been in that magic glass. She thought of Marguerite and Garth. Lovely Marguerite, loved by Garth . . . the pair of them taking delight in each other's beauty. Lovely and loved, thought Adela.

"Truly," said Hortensia, "my heart aches for you when I think of you among all the pretty girls I invited to my party. I suppose you dressed up in your best clothes, thinking that would help somehow. I suppose someone told you that you looked nice in blue."

Adela couldn't help it. Her eyes filled with tears again. She could not wipe them away, and they rolled down her cheeks.

"And here you are now," said Hortensia, "a weed among the pretty flowers in my garden . . ."

A weed among flowers. Was it regret that Adela felt then? Regret that she wasn't pretty enough to be in Hortensia's garden?

Oh, but that was wrong. She didn't want that!

Or did she? Perhaps she did want to be a flower . . . to be lovely and loved.

And then it was happening! Adela could feel her feet digging into the ground, pushing down into the soil. Her arms raised themselves up, and she saw that they were green! They were flattening, splitting, stretching out in all directions, turning into broad leaves with curves and spiny points! And still her feet were digging into the ground, her legs twisting together as they drove downward. "Stop!" she remembered to say. Only her voice was so tiny. And she was so tiny. She was shrinking away. Her head was becoming smaller, her hair shooting outward in a brilliant yellow crown. This is what it's like, she thought as her vision blurred. This is what it's like to be a flower.

And then, just as it occurred to her that being a flower was not what she wanted, everything went dark, and Adela thought of nothing at all.

chapter 22
PULLING WEEDS

Krazo was hiding under the wheelbarrow. He was watching and listening to Hortensia and thinking of a cat. There was a big gray tabby that lurked around one of the farmyards he visited, and Krazo had once seen it creep up on a mouse. The mouse had seen the cat; Krazo had thought it would run away, but the mouse had simply stood there, staring at the cat until it was too late to run.

Now it was too late for the princess.

Hortensia leaned over to touch her new flower. Krazo, remembering the silver key, held his breath. But Hortensia stood up, empty-handed, and Krazo saw the same satisfied look he had seen on the face of that farmyard cat. "Don't you worry, my dear," Hortensia said to the flower. "I'll be sure to tell your friend Garth to look for you in the morning."

Krazo waited for her to go inside before he searched for the key. He found it hidden among the flower's long, toothed leaves. He tugged at the chain, but it was caught. He tugged harder and very nearly ripped the plant apart before he caught himself. He jumped back, watching the plant's yellow flowers snap upright. They swayed and grew still, standing alert above the plant's green leaves, as if they expected him to say something.

"Princess?" said Krazo.

He had never given much thought to the flowers in Hortensia's garden. *My garden girls,* Hortensia called them, as if she owned them. As she now owned the princess. Because the flower *was* the princess. The princess was the flower. The princess was, as she had put it herself, *under a spell.*

Krazo looked at her. Even if he managed to pull the chain out of her leaves without harming her, what good would it do him? He couldn't dig up the treasure himself. "Princess?" he said again. He stood there for a long time. He waited until the lights in the house went out. And then, because there was nothing else he could do, he went home to bed.

He didn't sleep well. For one thing, his nest was too crowded for comfort. The belt buckle kept poking him, and the coral beads clacked against one another whenever he stirred. For another thing, his roof was gone. He wasn't used to sleeping in the open air. But the worst thing of all was that Krazo dreamed about the woman again. This time he dreamed that he was showing her his treasures, only there were far more than he had ever had before—a shower of diamonds and emeralds and rubies pouring from his hands into hers. "They're for you!" he said proudly. "This one here belonged to a princess," he added, showing her the necklace with the blue stone.

The woman raised her dark eyes. "Oh, Neddy, you must have stolen them!" she said. The tears were rolling down her face, and Krazo knew that he was the cause of them.

"I didn't!" he cried.

"Why, Neddy? Why must you steal when you know it's wrong?"

He woke up shivering. It was nearly dawn — he could tell by the light filtering through the leaves. He waited for the ache in his heart to subside and waited for the dream to fade from his mind.

Only it didn't entirely. The sun rose, the day was here, and the pain in his breast eased a bit, but Krazo could not stop thinking about the woman. She had spoken to him. She had called him Neddy, just as if it were his name, as if she knew him. And the way she had cried! As if he had never brought her anything but sorrow and disappointment. But how could that be, when it was clear that he had wanted to make her happy?

Krazo closed his eyes, bringing to mind the image of the jewels pouring from his hands into hers.

Hands. Was it only the dream that made him feel as if he knew what it was like to have them? Krazo stretched his wings, trying to imagine his feathers as fingers. He remembered what the princess had said to him: *You might be under a spell. . . .*

He opened his eyes. Was it possible? Could it be that

he was enchanted? "Neddy," he murmured, searching inside himself for some inkling of who he might once have been, until a noise tugged at his attention. Someone was singing down on the lawn. Krazo knew who it was: Hortensia's new gardener. The man had sung yesterday morning as well.

Krazo hopped out of his nest, landed on a branch below, then dropped down and down until he reached the ground. By then the gardener had stopped singing. He was standing by the wheelbarrow, staring at something in the grass. The man crouched down, and Krazo saw what had caught his eye.

The princess.

Now the gardener was standing up again. He was digging through the clutter in the wheelbarrow. Krazo watched as he pulled out a long metal rod with a wooden handle on one end and a forked blade on the other. The gardener knelt down beside the princess and drove the rod into the ground.

"Stop!" called Krazo.

The man looked around. As Krazo came toward him, he pulled out the rod and shook it at him. "Get off, you!" he threatened.

Krazo drew back, watching as the man pushed the rod into the ground again. He wiggled it back and forth, pushing on the wooden handle like a lever, until the princess popped out of the ground. Dirt flew from her roots as the gardener tossed her into the wheelbarrow. He tossed the rod in as well and stood up, brushing his hands on his trousers. Then, resuming his song, he picked up the handles of the wheelbarrow and started off.

"Stop!" Krazo said again. He flew toward the wheelbarrow. He landed on its rim. The princess was lying on top of the pruning saw. He barely noticed the silver key still twined among her leaves. "Where are you taking her?" he demanded.

The gardener scratched his head. "Where am I taking who?"

"The princess!" Krazo leaped down beside her.

"Do you mean that dandelion? Rubbish heap, I guess. Lady Hortensia told me I must kill all the weeds I found this morning. Say! You're that talking magpie Miss Adela told me about. I guess she was right about something, anyway."

"You killed her?" said Krazo.

"Who?"

Krazo leaned toward the princess.

"The dandelion? I should think so! Lucky I got to it before it went to seed!" said the gardener.

The princess didn't look dead. Her leaves, sprouting up from her dirt-encrusted taproot, were crisp and green and speckled with dew. Krazo could smell her grassy, springlike scent.

"I can't wait to tell Lady Hortensia," said the gardener. "She said only last night she'd give me a kiss for every weed I pulled!"

So the princess is dead, thought Krazo. She was dead, and it was Hortensia who had killed her, just as surely as if she had dug her up herself. In fact, Hortensia would probably tell him all about it later today. She would probably laugh about it. Krazo had never understood her laughter before. He didn't fully understand it now. But as he thought of the satisfied look he had seen on Hortensia's face, the same look he had seen on the face of that barnyard cat, it seemed to him that Hortensia's laughter must be a cruel thing.

"I don't suppose you know where I could find more dandelions," said the gardener.

Krazo looked up.

"I was just thinking about getting some more kisses from my lady."

The idea came so fast to Krazo it nearly knocked him over.

"I don't know about dandelions," he said. "But I do know something she wants killed. Follow me."

chapter 23

ONLY TREASURE

"Are you sure she wants this cut down?" The gardener brushed his fingers against one of the blooms on the rose tree.

"Yes!" Krazo lied.

The gardener cast a look at the debris scattered across the grass — the remains of the princess's battle with the rose tree. "Well," he said, still sounding dubious, "it does look as if it's shedding leaves and petals. But other than that —"

"It's what she wants! And then there's some digging. . . ."

"I'm good at digging. Maybe I ought to start with that."

"Tree first!" Krazo insisted. "Then dig!"

"All right, then." The gardener leaned over the wheelbarrow and pulled out the pruning saw. "This should work fine, but I'd better have a pair of gloves." He began to dig among the other tools. He picked up the princess and tossed her to the ground.

Krazo hopped over to her. When the gardener had killed the rose tree, he would show him the silver key. He would tell him to dig up the box. And then — would there be treasure inside it? Or, as the princess had promised, would there be something better than treasure? Something that would destroy Hortensia?

"Here we go!" said the gardener. He stood up, holding a pair of leather gloves. He put them on, knelt down beside the rose tree, and laid the blade against the trunk. But before he could begin sawing, a tree branch swatted his arm.

"Ouch!" The gardener fell backward. "Pesky thing," he growled. He grabbed the branch with a gloved hand and laid the blade against the trunk again. "Ouch!" he bellowed as another branch slapped him in the face. He jumped to his feet and touched his cheek, noting the blood there. He stared openmouthed at the tree, whose branches were drawn back like arms ready to let loose in a fight.

"Well, I never! You'd almost think it knew what I was going to do!" The gardener took a step forward, and the tree reacted, swiping one of its branches through the air so quickly that he barely had time to jump out of the way. He turned to the magpie. "No wonder my lady wants this cut down!"

Frowning, the gardener jabbed at the tree. It lashed out with a branch, but this time he was ready. He seized the branch and sliced it off with one decisive blow of his saw. The tree lashed out again, and the gardener sliced again. "Ha!" he said with a grin.

Now the tree picked up its attack, lashing out with two and three branches at a time. The gardener fought back, gathering the branches into one gloved hand and using the blade in his other hand to hack through them. Krazo joined in, too, flying at the tree, tearing apart the blooms with his beak and claws.

Finally, there was only one branch left. "Take *that!*" said the gardener as he sawed it from the trunk. He threw it on the ground and pulled off his gloves. He took out his handkerchief and dabbed at the cut on his cheek. "She ought to give me a kiss now, for sure!" he said.

But Krazo was already dragging aside the branches. "Time to dig," he said.

"Right!" The gardener picked up the shovel and looked at the spot Krazo showed him. "You're sure this is where she wants me to do it?"

"Yes!"

"Because if she wants to plant something, I'd say it's better to dig a little more out of the way —"

"Just dig!" Krazo was beginning to worry. Though it was still early morning, Hortensia *could* be awake now. What if she showed up before they were finished?

The gardener began to dig, and Krazo hopped back and forth in agitation. His worries increased as the hole deepened. Shouldn't the gardener have found the box already? What if this wasn't the right spot? What if Hortensia had dug it up and moved it?

And then, *Clink!*

The gardener stopped digging. He knelt down and reached into the hole. "Look at this!" He pulled the box out of the hole and shook the dirt off. "There's something rattling inside!" He tried to open the box. "It's locked!"

The princess lay half buried beneath a branch. Krazo seized her by the taproot and dragged her across the grass. "Here's the key!" he said.

"Well, I'll be! How did that get there?" The gardener dropped the box and picked up the princess. "It's caught," he muttered. He worked at the chain with his fingers, pulling it down over the taproot. "Got it!" He tossed the princess aside, then picked up the box again. "What do you know? It fits!" he marveled as he turned the key. Then he lifted the lid, and his eyes grew wide.

"Let me see! Let me see!" Krazo demanded.

The gardener held up a large heart-shaped stone. "Looks like a ruby!" he said, watching it catch the light. "It must be worth a fortune!"

Krazo's heart sank. The princess was wrong. It was only treasure.

Then a movement behind him caught his eye. "What are you doing?" shrieked a familiar voice.

Krazo whirled around to see Hortensia standing at the entrance to the enclosed yard. Her fists were clenched at her sides, and her face was contorted with fury. He dove under the wheelbarrow.

The gardener jumped to his feet. "My lady!" he said.

"I've cut down the rose tree, and I've dug the hole you wanted."

Krazo peeked out from behind a wheel.

"Give me my heart!" Hortensia held out her hand, palm open.

The gardener's smile evaporated. "Wh-what?"

"My heart! Give it to me!"

"I don't know what you mean, my lady."

"The ruby, you fool! Give me the ruby!"

She snatched it from him. She cradled it in her hands. "How did you find it?" she demanded.

"It was a magpie! It said you wanted—"

"Krazo!" Hortensia's eyes flashed. "I'll tear his wings off! I'll slit his throat! I'll boil him alive!"

Krazo shrank back out of sight.

"I—I cut down the rose tree, j-just as you wanted, my lady," the gardener stammered. "And I pulled up a dandelion. You said you'd give me a kiss."

"You fool! Do you have any idea how precious this is?"

Precious, thought Krazo. He looked at the princess—at her wilted leaves. She was dead. Hortensia had killed her, and the only thing she cared about was treasure.

Suddenly his brain felt hot. All he could see was red. His head was filled with fire. He wasn't even aware that he was moving, that he was flying up in the air . . .

"There you are!" snarled Hortensia, and Krazo could feel her fury crackling through his mind. But his own anger was greater. He attacked, flapping his wings and scratching at her face with his claws. Hortensia raised her arms, trying to fend him off. He grabbed her hand with his claws. She shrieked and cursed, trying to shake him off, but Krazo bit her wrist and held on. The gardener was shouting; his hands grabbed Krazo, but still the magpie kept his grip on Hortensia. He bit down and dug his claws into her flesh again and again until at last the ruby fell to the ground. Only then did Krazo let go. Hortensia grasped for the stone, but Krazo was faster. He didn't want the ruby, but if this was what she cared about — if this was her most prized possession — he wanted to crush it. He would carry it high in the air and drop it in the sea. He would smash it against a rock. He would destroy it! His claws encircled the ruby —

"No!" screamed Hortensia.

And it shattered into pieces.

"My heart!" she wailed.

chapter 24
THE FLOWERS

There are any number of things a flower can feel: the warmth of the sun, the chill of night coming on, the dampness of the soil, even the tiny nibble of a caterpillar. But it feels these things without knowing what it feels. It feels without awareness.

That was how it was for the flower that was Adela. It felt itself being pulled from the earth. It felt itself wilting under the heat of the sun. The flower was dying, but it could not know that it was dying. It could not know anything at all.

And then something happened.

The flower that was Adela felt an impulse to move. In itself, this was not so unusual. All flowers are compelled to move in response to their environment. They turn their leaves to follow the sun across the sky, close their blooms at sunset, dig their roots down into the soil in search of water. But this impulse was different, because it came into being without any outside stimulus. The flower that was Adela simply felt the need to stretch. It could feel itself stretching — roots, stems, leaves, and blossoms. And the more it stretched, the greater the need became, until it was no longer a need but a desire. I want, thought the flower. I want, thought Adela, and she opened her eyes.

"Miss Adela?" Garth was leaning over her. He looked worried. "Are you all right?"

She tried to answer him but couldn't. She sat up and swayed from dizziness, then leaned into Garth's steadying arm. She closed her eyes, trying to reconcile the lingering feeling of being a flower with the familiar and yet unfamiliar feeling of being herself again. Arms and legs, hands and feet, fingers and toes! Ears for hearing, mouth for talking, eyes for seeing!

She opened her eyes again, and her breath caught in her throat. There, looming over them, was Hortensia, her hands reaching and grasping at the air, her mouth open in an agonized cry.

Only the cry did not come. Hortensia loomed without moving a muscle. In fact, it was not Hortensia at all; it was a white marble statue, perfect in every detail.

"I don't know what happened," said Garth, staring up at it. "She was standing there and — and suddenly she turned to stone. It started at her hands, and then it went right up her arms and into her face. It was like watching her turn into a corpse!" He shuddered. "And then the walls disappeared, and I turned around, and there you were, Miss Adela! Only it wasn't you! You were —"

"A flower?" she finished.

"Yes!" said Garth, his eyes wide. "You were a dandelion . . . But only at first . . . because your head popped out of the stem, and then your arms and your legs!"

A dandelion, Adela thought wryly. Then, "Where are we?" she wondered aloud. She remembered standing beside the fountain on Hortensia's front lawn. Now the fountain was nowhere to be seen, and there were people — hundreds of them — chattering and clamoring, some of them even crying. She had just taken in the fact that they were all women when she heard a groan behind her. Turning, Adela saw a man lying curled up on the ground next to Garth's wheelbarrow. The man gave another groan and rolled over onto his back.

"He's hurt!" she said.

They hurried to his side, and Adela saw that he was young. He can't be much older than I am, she thought. His hand was bleeding. She touched it, and his eyes fluttered open.

"Princess!" he said, gripping her hand. "You're all right!"

Did she know him? Adela knew she had not met the young man at the garden party. And if not there, then where? His eyes seemed to look right inside her. They were brown, almost as dark as his hair. They were beautiful eyes, and she was suddenly acutely aware of the touch of his hand on hers.

"Who are you?" she asked. She tried to pull away, but he didn't let go.

"My name's Ned — Edward . . ." He tried to sit up, and she had to help him, just as Garth had helped her.

Edward looked at the marble statue. "Is she — is she *destroyed?*" he asked.

"I think so," said Adela.

"You were right. It wasn't treasure in the box."

"What box?"

"The one she buried. It had a ruby in it. Only it couldn't have been a ruby, because it shattered when I grabbed it. It's just like that flask, isn't it?"

Suddenly Adela knew who he was. "You're the magpie!" She stared at him, astonished to find her speculation about its being under a spell come true.

Edward's expression was anxious. She smiled to put him at ease. And blushed. She couldn't help it. He was still holding her hand, and the words *enchanted prince* had flitted through her mind.

"Your Highness?"

Adela gave a start. Her hand slipped from Edward's, and she looked up to see Marguerite making her way toward them. Garth jumped to his feet, hurrying forward to help her through the crowd.

"What is going on?" asked Marguerite. "Who are all these women?"

Adela looked around, and for the first time, she fully understood all that had happened. "They're Hortensia's garden!" she said. "They're the flowers."

chapter 25

A BEAUTIFUL PERSON

The flowers had vanished. So had the walls of Hortensia's garden. There were only several hundred extremely pretty and very confused young women to show that it had ever existed. Some of them listened as Adela told Marguerite and Garth what had happened. Edward went on to explain that Hortensia had been holding garden parties for years — inviting beautiful young women and turning them into flowers, inviting handsome young men and turning them into her servants.

"How many years?" Adela asked, remembering the servant she had seen wearing old-fashioned clothing.

But Edward couldn't remember. None of the guests could. Finally, someone asked what year it was. When Adela told them, Edward turned pale. Some of the women listening burst into tears. One of them who looked no older than fifteen or sixteen revealed that she had been an amaryllis for more than twenty years.

And so the dreadful tale spread through the crowd.

"What a horrible woman that Hortensia was!" said Marguerite. "You were very brave to stand up to her, Garth!"

He looked sheepish. "All I did was chop down a tree and dig up a box. And I never would have done that if it hadn't been for the magpie — I mean, *him.*"

He nodded toward Edward, who looked as uncomfortable as Garth at the suggestion that he had done anything heroic. "All I did — except maybe right at the end — was try to steal your jewelry, Princess. I'm sorry about that."

Edward's apology — and his obvious remorse — made Adela like him even more than she already did. She wondered who he was and where he was from. He clearly wasn't an enchanted prince. His accent suggested that he came from one of the poorer neighborhoods of one of the coastal cities; he slurred his words together like one of the gardeners at home. As Cecile would put it, Edward wasn't *of the gentry*. Which meant, for example, that he didn't know he should say *Your Highness* when he spoke to her. Not that she minded. She felt a small thrill when he called her *Princess*. She hoped he didn't notice that she turned pink whenever he looked her way.

The mention of jewelry had caused Marguerite to realize that hers was missing. "The diamond necklace. And the earrings! Where are they?"

Adela was pretty sure that she knew where the necklace was. She jumped to her feet. "Wait here! I'll be right back."

But Edward followed her. "I'm the one who took the earrings," he said. "They're in my — that is, they're up in a tree on the front lawn."

But there were no trees on the front lawn, for they had vanished along with the garden. Hortensia's house was gone, too. Her servants, looking every bit as confused — and as beautiful, Adela noted — as the former flowers, were wandering about in what she guessed had been its approximate location. She soon found

Hortensia's pile of stolen jewelry, lying untouched in the grass. "My guess is that you'll find the contents of your nest on the ground as well, Edward," she said.

He went to look and, sure enough, returned within minutes with a smaller hoard. He handed the jewels to Adela with yet another shamefaced apology.

"You were a magpie! You couldn't help what you were doing," she told him. "I can't say the same for Hortensia."

Adela retrieved the diamond necklace from the pile on the ground and put it in her pocket along with the diamond earrings and blue stone pendant from Edward. She made a basket of her skirt and raked all the other jewels into it.

Then she looked around. "People are already leaving, aren't they?"

Indeed, the numbers of the crowd were dwindling.

"I don't think anyone but Marguerite cares much about jewelry right now," said Adela. "Perhaps the best thing to do is to take all this with us. My father can issue some sort of decree inviting people to come and claim what they've lost."

•   •   •

When they rejoined Garth and Marguerite, the pair of them were discussing how to get home. "What about the carriage?" Garth asked Adela.

"I don't think it's here anymore," she said. "I looked for it yesterday, but I couldn't find any stables. I hope Axel is all right."

"Is that your coachman?" said Edward. "Hortensia sent him home the day you came to the party."

Adela was relieved. "So he's all right! And if he came home without us, Father already knows something's wrong. He'll have sent someone to find us."

But Edward shook his head. "She put your coachman under a spell. He won't remember a thing about anything he saw here. And Hortensia sent letters to your families about the rest of you — magic letters to keep them from worrying and to make them forget about you over time. I know because I delivered yours, Princess."

"But we've only been gone a few days," said Adela. "They couldn't forget about us that quickly, could they?"

"Maybe not. You're lucky if that's true."

Adela had a flash of insight. "Are you worried about your parents, Edward?"

He nodded, this time avoiding her gaze. "My mother . . ." he began. "She didn't want me to come here. When I got the invitation, she . . ." His voice trailed away.

Adela wasn't surprised to learn that Edward had been invited to a garden party. He was easily as handsome as the other men Hortensia had enchanted.

"I'm sure your mother will remember you when she sees you." But even as she said this, Adela could see a problem. She thought of the woman they had met earlier — more than twenty years of enchantment! How long had Edward been a magpie? What if his mother was an old woman now? Why, she might even be dead! Was that the reason he looked so worried?

"We'll have to walk home," said Garth, interrupting her thoughts. "That's what everyone else is doing. We'd better hurry if we want to get down the mountain before dark."

"You should come with us, Edward," said Adela, and immediately felt herself blushing.

But he was looking up at the statue of Hortensia, which loomed over them, its expression disturbingly lifelike. "What about her?" he said.

"She can't hurt anyone now," said Adela.

He didn't look convinced. "Are you sure she's dead?"

Garth reached out and touched Hortensia's marble hand. "Solid stone," he confirmed.

"Still . . ." Edward stared at the statue for a moment. Then, with a look of determination, he gave it a shove.

The statue didn't budge.

Adela thought she must be feeling what Edward was, because suddenly, more than anything, she wanted to see the statue knocked down. She stood next to him and pushed. Garth and Marguerite joined in. At last the statue toppled, hitting the ground with a powerful crash that broke Hortensia into pieces.

"I can't imagine her coming back from that," said Adela.

Garth leaned over to look at Hortensia's face. "It's a shame, isn't it? To be so very beautiful and so very wicked?"

Edward frowned. "I don't think she was beautiful at all," he said. "A beautiful person is someone you want to look at because they're good and kind. Because being with them makes you happy. I'll be happy if I never see Hortensia again."

He looked at Adela. "Now, Princess. If you really meant I should come with you, I'd like that."

But Adela couldn't speak. She was thinking about what he had said — that a beautiful person was someone who was good and kind, who made you happy.

She thought of what Hortensia had said, that people loved beauty most of all.

But they don't, thought Adela. They love what's inside a person. That's what makes people worthy of love.

Edward was watching her, and she wondered what he saw. Did he see someone whom Hortensia had chosen to turn into a dandelion — a weed? Or did he see someone more beautiful than that — someone who was brave and kind?

Because when she looked at him, Adela felt as if she could see more than the handsome face that had won him an invitation to Hortensia's garden party. She felt as if she could see inside Edward.

And what she saw was beautiful.

chapter 26
WAGON RIDE

He knew what it was like to be a bird — to spread his wings and escape into the air. And now, after so long, he knew what it was like to be himself again. Edward's mind stirred with conflicting memories and impressions.

It was dark now. The sun had set hours ago, and they were at a farm. He had walked down the mountain with the princess, the gardener, and the girl with the diamonds — *Garth and Marguerite*, he reminded himself. The princess had just hired a horse and wagon from the farmer, paying him with the diamond necklace she had loaned Marguerite. It seemed like the sort of thing a princess *would* do, paying for something with diamonds.

"I'll drive," said Garth.

"I'll sit with you," said Marguerite.

"Do you mind riding in back with me, Edward?" asked the princess.

She was *Your Highness,* or maybe *Miss Adela,* or maybe simply *Adela.* He didn't know what to call her. He shook his head. "No. I don't mind, Princess."

She hoisted a cloth bundle into the wagon. It was the gardener's coat, wrapped around the jewelry Hortensia had stolen. Edward had thought of offering to help the princess and her father return the jewels to their owners. After all, he had visited most of the homes of Hortensia's guests to deliver their invitations; he was sure he would remember which person had worn which jewel. But it bothered him that he remembered that particular detail about each guest — a detail only a thief would recall. What would the princess think of him if she knew he was a thief?

She climbed into the wagon, turning so that she sat with her legs dangling out the back. Edward pulled himself up beside her.

"It's chilly, isn't it?" she said, rubbing her arms. "I

suppose Hortensia must have enchanted the weather along with everything else. This feels more like October than the past couple of days."

Edward pulled off his jacket. "Here. Take this."

"But you'll be cold!"

"I'll be fine," he said as he draped the jacket around her shoulders, adding, when she started to protest, "I'm used to being outside. That's what thirty years as a magpie will do for a person."

"Thirty years! Oh, Edward!"

He hadn't meant to tell her that. How would she feel about him, knowing that he'd spent more years as a magpie than he'd spent as a man? "It's all right," he said quickly.

"But your mother!" said the princess.

He could tell from her voice that she understood his fear: that he'd been away too long. He was trying not to think how sick his mother had been when he'd left home. It would be a miracle if she were still alive. "I'll find her," he said, feeling little of the confidence he tried to put in his voice. He shivered.

"You *are* cold!" said the princess. "Don't you want your jacket back?"

"I'm only tired."

"Me, too," she agreed. "I don't know what my brain was doing when I was a dandelion, but it couldn't have been sleeping. We should try to rest."

She pushed herself back into the wagon and lay down. He did, too, as if it were something he did every day — lying in the back of a wagon with a princess. He crossed his arms behind his head and looked up at the stars.

But he wasn't really tired. His mind was too busy thinking. The princess wanted him to come home with her. "Father can help you find your mother," she had told him. "And in the meantime, you can stay with me — I mean, us." Just as if it were the most ordinary thing in the world — a thief being the guest of a princess. Except she didn't know he was a thief. All she knew was that Hortensia had turned him into a magpie; she didn't know why.

He lay there, thinking and listening. In the front of the wagon, the gardener and the girl with the diamonds were murmuring to each other. *Lovebirds*, his mother would have called them. *They only have eyes for each other.*

Edward looked at the princess. She was lying on

her side, her head resting on one arm, her other arm bent in front of her. Her eyes were closed. He turned toward her. He watched her for a while and listened to the soft voices of the lovebirds. At last he reached out and pushed his hand under hers.

Her eyes opened. She didn't speak, but her fingers curled around his, and he remembered what it had been like, coming out of the dream that his magpie life had been. He remembered her holding his hand and looking down at him.

"I thought you were dead," he said.

"What?"

"When you were a flower. The gardener told me you were dead. He dug you out of the ground, roots and all."

The princess smiled. "That wouldn't kill me. Garth could have transplanted me, and I would have been just fine. Not that he would have. There isn't a gardener in the world that likes dandelions."

"I like them," said Edward. To be sure, he had never given them a thought until yesterday. But he knew he would never again look at a dandelion without thinking of the princess.

She laughed. "They're weeds!"

"If I had a garden, it would be only dandelions. Nothing else."

He loved to hear her laugh. "You don't know anything about gardens!" she said.

"Only magic ones," he agreed. "You'll have to tell me about the other kind. Why do you like them so much?"

He knew she loved gardens; it was the reason she had come to Hortensia's party. But he also knew that Hortensia loved gardens, and it confused him that the princess should love them as well. She was as different from Hortensia as a person could be.

Her brow furrowed as she considered his question. "Besides the fact that gardens are beautiful to look at, you mean? I suppose it's all the work that goes into making them: planning and planting, weeding and pruning. I like all of those things. But I also love to learn about new methods for planting and new types of plants. I want to travel all over the world and talk to other gardeners. I want to collect plants and bring them back home to see if I can grow them myself."

"I wish I could go—" Edward started to say, then stopped himself. Because what he wished was that he could go with her. Because he would give anything to go on just as he was now, talking to her and being close to her. But how could that ever happen?

You'll be a thief forever, Hortensia had told him, and she was probably right about that. Even if he felt no temptation to steal now, it could only be a matter of time before he slipped back into his old ways.

He recalled something his mother had once said to him: *You're a handsome boy, Neddy. You can smile at a girl—you can look at her, say a few words—and steal her heart. You need to be careful not to hurt a girl that way.* Even with love, it seemed he could be a thief. And wasn't that what he was doing now? Stealing love—telling the princess things that made her smile and want to hold his hand . . .

Except that I would never hurt her, he thought.

But maybe he would. He had hurt his mother. He hadn't meant to, but it had happened anyway because of what he was. . . .

Steal from me, and you'll be a thief forever.

He might love the princess, but how could he expect her to love someone like him?

"Go where, Edward?" she murmured drowsily, her eyes drooping.

"Nowhere," he said too quickly.

But she didn't notice. She was falling asleep. He felt her grip on his hand loosen. At the front of the wagon, the lovebirds had grown quiet. The girl with the diamonds was leaning against the gardener. His arm was around her, and their heads bobbed in rhythm with the horse's steady pace as if they, too, were asleep.

He lay there watching the princess, pretending that he could see her dreams and that they were the same as his own — the two of them on a road together, the two of them learning about gardens, planting gardens full of dandelions and other flowers. And all the while, he would know that she could see him for who he wanted to be — not for who he had been.

He held this dream in his mind for a long time, until at last he let it go. He slipped his hand out from under hers. The princess sighed without waking and moved her hand under her cheek.

Then, as quiet as only a thief could be, Edward tucked the bundle of jewels under his arm, crept to the edge of the wagon, and slipped silently to the ground. He watched the wagon roll away, waiting for it to disappear before he began walking in the other direction.

chapter 27
THE KING IVAL MEDAL

"We're home!" said Garth.

Adela opened her eyes and saw that it was still dark. She wasn't walking through a sunlit garden with Edward; she had only been dreaming. She sat up and saw that the wagon was stopped at the palace gates, waiting while the guards opened them.

"Wait! Where's Edward?" said Adela as the horse began to move forward.

"Whoa!" Garth pulled on the reins.

Marguerite turned around. "I thought he was back there with you."

"He was. But I fell asleep. He must have fallen out!"

"Edward!" bellowed Garth.

"Edward?" called Adela.

They waited, but there was no response.

Garth called to the guard, "Did you see anyone climb out of the wagon as we came up?"

"No, sir."

"Do you suppose he's hurt?" Adela pictured Edward lying unconscious somewhere on the road behind them.

"We'd have heard him if he fell. I'm sure he must have climbed out," said Garth.

"But he wouldn't have left without telling us!" Then Adela noticed something. "Oh, no! The jewels are gone!"

Maybe the bundle had fallen out of the wagon *with* Edward. Or maybe Edward had seen the bundle fall and had climbed out to retrieve it. Maybe it had fallen open, the jewels spilled all over the road. By the time he had gathered them up, the wagon was out of sight. But even that seemed unlikely. The wagon couldn't have been going that fast. Edward could have caught up. He could have called out to them.

"He's stolen the jewels," said Garth. "Your magpie friend is a thief, Miss Adela."

"But that doesn't make any sense!" She reached into her pocket and felt the diamond earrings and the necklace with the blue stone. Edward had seemed so upset about having taken them from her. She couldn't imagine him stealing anything. He couldn't be a thief!

When they reached the palace, the steward sent a servant to summon the king and queen. Adela's father and stepmother appeared soon after, looking bleary-eyed and surprised to see the partygoers.

"Darling!" said Cecile, throwing her arms around Marguerite. "I thought you had decided to stay at Lady Hortensia's! She wrote and told us how pleased she was to have you. 'Like having a beautiful daisy added to her garden,' she said. What ever made you—?" But Cecile had finally noticed Adela. She drew back with a shocked expression. "My dear girl! What has happened to you? You're covered with scratches! And your hair! Your clothes!"

"I had a bit of a fight with a rose tree," said Adela.

Cecile clucked her tongue. "Really, Adela, only you would think to go to a garden party and actually try to garden. I'm sure Lady Hortensia must have been terribly displeased. Though I must say, I don't think much of her for sending you home at such a late hour, and in such a state!"

"She didn't send us home," said Marguerite. "Oh, Cecile, you are *not* going to believe what we have to tell you!"

At first, Adela let Marguerite explain what had happened to them, but she mangled the story badly, relating everything out of sequence and leaving out important details. Edward, for example, had no important part in her version of events. He was only "that magpie boy who stole all the jewelry." So Adela had to tell the story all over again from beginning to end; when she finished, her father actually gave a derisive snort. "You must be joking, Adela!"

And Cecile added, "I can't say it's very funny, waking us up at this hour with such nonsense."

The king and queen might never have believed them, but for the fact that within days, strange reports began to arrive from around the kingdom. It seemed that Hortensia's other guests were returning home. Their family members, having forgotten about them for so many years, were now shocked to find their loved ones restored to memory. Stranger still, their loved ones were often impossibly young! There were too many such stories to ignore. "It doesn't make any sense," Adela's father complained. "I have a report here of a man who says he's thirty-seven years old. He claims his older sister has come home, and she's only nineteen years old."

At last Adela suggested that the king seek the advice of Dr. Sophus. She had already told her tutor about her adventure with Hortensia, and she knew her father thought highly of his opinions. ("I know the man is brilliant," the king would say, "because I can never understand what he's talking about.") Dr. Sophus pointed out to the king that the historical record was replete with examples of enchantments that involved curious temporal paradoxes similar to the ones being reported. Adela's father was — if not fully convinced — at least impressed.

"After Her Royal Highness informed me of her adventure at Flower Mountain, I did a bit of poking around in the library," said Dr. Sophus. "I found several accounts of a beautiful witch who seems to have been active around the time your ancestor King Adalbert IV issued his famous anti-magic legislation. This witch — or Hortensia, as I believe she must later have come to be called—was very powerful from the start. She seems to have chased all other practicing magicians out of her territory. My guess is that after that, she rather successfully went into hiding and continued to practice her craft. We owe a great debt to Her Royal Highness for having the wits and courage to rid the kingdom of her."

From here, Dr. Sophus went on to convince the king, through gentle urging, that he ought to bestow the King Ival Medal for bravery upon his daughter.

"And Garth and Edward," Adela added. "I would still be a dandelion and Hortensia would still be enchanting people if not for them."

She had been thinking about Edward for days. Her mind had busied itself with various explanations for what could have happened to him. Maybe he and the jewelry really had fallen out of the wagon. Before Edward had been able to call out, a thief had attacked him, knocked him out, and stolen the jewels. By the time Edward had come to his senses, the wagon had disappeared. Now he was afraid to come forward because the jewels were missing. There was also a variation on this scenario that Adela didn't like to entertain: that the thief had slit Edward's throat.

"Edward?" Her father wore a blank expression.

"I believe Her Highness is referring to the young man who, until recently, was an enchanted magpie," said Dr. Sophus.

"Ah! That fellow! Come, now, Adela, you can't expect me to award a medal to a thief."

Adela protested, "He couldn't have stolen the jewelry! He wouldn't have!" But she wasn't going to tell her father her reasons for believing in Edward's innocence. Because he had told her he liked dandelions? Because he had held her hand? Because she had felt as if she could see inside him? The reasons would sound foolish if she put them into words.

"Well," said the king, "even so, I don't see how I can award him a medal. He's not here, is he?"

No, Adela thought, he isn't.

chapter 28

CECILE'S IDEA

The next morning, Adela rose early, had breakfast in the kitchen, and was outdoors by sunrise. She had been neglecting her garden since coming home. Now she set to work digging up the beds where she wanted to plant bulbs. She tried hard to focus her mind on the task. She punched holes in the ground with her spade, dropped in the bulbs, and pushed the dirt over them. Tulips, daffodils, hyacinths — she had to keep reminding herself what she had planted where. By midmorning, she felt successful. Her arms and shoulders ached, she was filthy, and she hadn't thought about Edward for several hours.

She cleaned up and changed her clothes, then hurried off to her lessons with Dr. Sophus. The first hour was geometry constructions. Adela liked using a compass and straightedge; she drew a series of perpendicular bisectors and pictured a garden based on the pattern of intersecting arcs and segments. After geometry came geography, which was interesting because it involved maps, and she could think about where she would go on her plant-collecting expedition. Unfortunately, Dr. Sophus began the lesson with a map showing the kingdom's coastal communities. Adela couldn't help but think of Edward. Was she right about his accent? Had he headed home to find his mother? But if so, why had he taken the jewels?

To avoid further speculation, she distracted Dr. Sophus with a question about the islands located several hundred miles off the coast. Was the climate tropical or semitropical? Dr. Sophus put away the first map and pulled out a more detailed map of the islands. He launched into a lecture on their flora and fauna, which was fine until Adela fell into a reverie in which she imagined sailing to the islands with Edward. Stop it! she told herself.

At lunchtime, Adela ate in the nursery with her

brother, Henry: cheese sandwiches, apples, and vanilla custard — his favorite foods at present. She entertained him by letting him pretend to be a bear. He growled as he ate his food, shoving it rudely into his mouth, much to the despair of his nanny. The game of bear went on after lunch because Cecile "wanted to discuss something" with the king and was too busy to bother with the usual embroidery lesson. Adela took on the role of a hunter. She chased Henry around the room, up and over the furniture, shooting at him with an imaginary bow and arrow. Henry fell to the ground again and again, roaring back to life each time. At last, laughing and gasping for breath, Adela suggested that he could be an enchanted bear who turned into a prince. "I don't want to be a prince!" shouted Henry, and let out another roar. Finally, to placate his nanny, Adela read her brother a story about King Ival that put him to sleep. The story wasn't "The Dog Princess," but it might as well have been, for almost as soon as Henry grew quiet, Adela's voice trailed off and her mind returned to thoughts of Edward. *If I had a garden, it would be only dandelions.* Why would he say such a thing if he didn't care about her? She thought she knew the answer. It was because he was teasing her—that was how beautiful boys like Edward talked to girls, even ones who weren't pretty. *A weed among the pretty flowers*—that was what Hortensia had called her.

Just before she turned me into a dandelion, thought Adela.

For tea, it was only Cecile, Adela, and Marguerite around the table in the queen's private sitting room. Her other ladies-in-waiting had been dismissed for the afternoon so that Cecile could share some exciting news.

"I've spoken to His Majesty," said the queen, "and he agrees with me that, in addition to receiving the King Ival Medal, Garth will also get a title and a monetary reward."

Marguerite gave a squeal and threw her arms around her sister. "Oh, Cecile! Thank you!"

"Don't let anyone ever accuse me of standing in the way of love," said Cecile. "I told His Majesty, 'Garth has gone head over heels for Marguerite, and she feels the same way about him. They are simply dying to get married. But Marguerite *is* your sister-in-law, and it will hardly do to have her marry a servant. There is only one solution to the problem, Adalbert, and that is to raise the boy up in the world.'" Cecile looked triumphant. "He's to be named an honorary Knight of the Realm, and he'll receive a bag of gold."

Sir Garth, brother-in-law to the queen. Life at the palace will never be the same again, thought Adela. She took a sip of her tea, marveling at Cecile's skills at manipulating the social world. First she had managed to marry the king, beating out princesses, duchesses, and ladies with far greater status than her own. Now she had arranged things so that her sister could marry the son of the head gardener without the least bit of scandal.

"And now for my other bit of news," said Cecile. "His Majesty's plans for awarding the King Ival Medal are what gave me the idea. We're going to have Adela's grand ball on the same day the medal is awarded—"

Adela opened her mouth to protest, but Cecile held up her hand.

"Now, then, Adela, you must listen to my plan before you say a word. I know you'll agree that I have your best interests at heart. Your father will award the medals at the ball, which is going to be a masquerade party with a garden theme: the ladies will come dressed as their favorite flowers!"

"What about the men?" asked Marguerite.

"We'll have them dress as bees and grasshoppers and birds — garden creatures, you know," said Cecile. "Perhaps even magpies," she added.

Adela stared, dumbfounded.

"The ball will be a grand celebration of your and Garth's triumph over Hortensia, Adela," Cecile continued. "But it will also be a celebration of *you* — and the fact that you are, in your own way, coming into bloom."

Adela choked on her tea. "Coming into bloom?"

Marguerite, meanwhile, was practically bouncing up and down with excitement. "I'm going to go as a daisy! It's Garth's favorite flower, and I can just imagine my gown. It will be white with tiny daisies embroidered all over it." She frowned. "Or maybe the skirt should look like petals."

Adela shuddered, remembering what she had seen at Hortensia's garden. Surely her stepmother couldn't be serious. "Enough!" she said, setting her teacup down firmly. "Cecile, can't you see how wildly inappropriate this theme is? Hundreds of girls were turned into flowers by a *witch*. I can't imagine any of them" — Adela avoided looking at Marguerite — "wanting to relive that experience.

"Besides," she added, trying to compose herself. "I've already told you I don't want to have a grand ball."

"Yes, dear," said Cecile. "But that was before you knew you would be receiving the King Ival Medal. Surely you don't want your guests to come all this way and not treat them to a bit of a celebration?"

"Please, Your Highness!" Marguerite implored.

Adela felt trapped. Was she really the only person who felt that such a ball was in poor taste? Obviously Marguerite felt differently. Maybe it was wrong to let her personal feelings interfere with Marguerite's happiness.

"All right," she agreed at last. She sat back in silence, listening to her stepmother and Marguerite chatter away about their various costume ideas. It wasn't long, however, before their conversation turned to Garth's good fortune and Marguerite's happiness and the possibility of having a wedding by the end of summer.

How quickly love had come for Marguerite and Garth! Adela couldn't help but feel a little envious.

What if she knew Edward would be at the ball? Would she, like Marguerite, look forward to surprising him with her costume? Would she actually enjoy dancing with him? Adela, who had never liked dancing in her life, had to admit that she might.

But Edward wouldn't be there, and it was foolish to imagine that he would. I need to concentrate on other things, Adela told herself. Like gardening and being awarded the King Ival Medal and my plans for the future.

Plans that wouldn't include anything as silly and distracting as love.

chapter 29

FROM RAGTOWN TO LAVENDER LANE

Edward was fighting off a feeling of panic. It had been some days since he had parted ways with the princess, and he was finally nearing his destination. He was going to find his mother. Or find out what had happened to her — whatever her fate might have been.

Ragtown, his old neighborhood, still looked the same as it had thirty years ago: narrow, crooked alleyways all tangled together like strips of dirty cloth. Even the people and the animals were variations on what he remembered: half-wild children shrieking at their games, worn-out parents shouting at them to stop their racket, dogs barking and snapping at his heels.

He was aware of eyes following him as he walked along his street. Not because anyone recognized him; too many years had passed for that. Instead, people were sizing up the stranger who had entered their midst, dressed in worn clothes that were long out of fashion but were still fancier than they were used to seeing in these parts. Edward shifted the bundle he was carrying from one arm to the other. Thirty years ago, there had been men here who would murder him for the jewels he carried; no doubt there were still men like that. There would also be those who would pay him for the jewels, dishonest dealers accustomed to working with thieves.

But that wasn't his business today. He stopped in front of a narrow three-story building no different from any of the others crowded together like rotten teeth. He glanced up, noting the small window on the top floor. The shutters were thrown open to let in the light — and the cold; few people here could afford the luxury of glass panes.

He knocked on the door.

He waited, then knocked again.

"Looking for Maud, are you?" said a voice behind him.

A bone-thin little girl with a sharp face was standing behind him. She was almost as dirty as the toddler she balanced on her hip.

Maud was the name of his mother's landlady. "Does she still live here?" he asked.

"Doesn't like to come out. She's half blind." The girl stepped past him and kicked open the door. "Oi! Maud! Someone to see you!" she bellowed. "Just go on in," she added.

Edward entered and closed the door quietly behind him. The hallway he found himself in was as dingy and depressing as ever, the only light coming from a window with a broken shutter at the top of a rickety flight of stairs. The shutter had been broken long ago; he knew because he had broken it himself, earning a clap on the ear from the landlady. It startled him to see so little changed. Was it possible that his mother might actually still live in the little room on the third floor?

"What do you want?" said a cross voice behind him.

He whirled around. Maud's body was crippled with age, her face as wrinkled as a mushroom, and her eyes frosted blue from cataracts. The only thing that hadn't changed was her scowl.

Edward explained that he was looking for a woman, who had lived on the top floor about thirty years before. When he described his mother, Maud's scowl became a sneer.

"That one! You mean the one that never paid her rent on time. Never *could* pay her rent after that worthless, thieving son of hers ran away and left her."

The panic was back — a sick feeling in the pit of his stomach. "Do you know what happened to her?" he asked.

Maud gave a snort. "Dead and buried would be my guess. Never did nothing but cough all day and night. But you'd have to ask the doctor that came and took her away."

"Doctor?" His mother couldn't afford a doctor.

"One of those charitable types from the hospital."

The hospital was clear across town, in a much better neighborhood than this one. "Is that where he took her?" asked Edward.

"How should I know?"

"Do you know his name?"

Another snort. "If I ever did know, I'm not likely to think of it after all this time. Who's asking, anyway?" Maud peered at him, as if she could see inside his mind with her disturbing blind eyes. As if she could see his shame.

He decided to go to the hospital. Maybe there would be a record of her there. Maybe he could even find the doctor who had helped her.

But as he headed away from the filthy streets of Ragtown, Maud's words rang in his ears: *Dead and buried would be my guess.*

He thought of the princess. He had made the right choice, leaving her to search for his mother on his own. Just imagine if she could hear what Maud had said of him: *Worthless, thieving son . . . ran away and left her.*

Edward wasn't sure he could bear having her know the truth about him, though a day did not pass when he didn't imagine the princess saying that none of it mattered, that he wasn't the same person he had been thirty years ago.

Perhaps it was even true. The treasures he carried didn't tempt him in the least. Shouldn't that mean something? *You'll be a thief forever*, Hortensia had told him, but shouldn't it matter that he no longer wanted to steal? Shouldn't it matter that he had already been punished — and that he wanted to make amends?

After he learned the truth about his mother, he was going to return the jewels in the bundle to their owners — the ones he could find, anyway. There were some pieces that he didn't recognize. Some of them may have belonged to Hortensia, or, more likely, they belonged to guests who had come to Flower Mountain before he had. He liked to imagine himself bringing these last treasures to the princess. "I've returned all the things I could," he would tell her. And she would say, "Oh, Edward!" as if she could see all the sorrow and regret and goodness inside him. And he would find out that it was possible, after all, for a princess to love a thief.

Edward turned onto the street with the hospital. He slowed his pace as he approached the gate, feeling the panic rise again. It didn't seem to make a difference how often he steeled himself to what he knew must be the truth about his mother. She was gone, and he would never be able to tell her the words he longed to say: *I'm sorry. I am so, so sorry.*

•   •   •

Inside the entrance of the stately building, a well-fed, bored-looking young man was sitting behind a desk marking a stack of ledgers.

Edward cleared his throat.

"Yes?"

"Are there any doctors here who make charitable visits to patients in Ragtown?"

The man made a face. "A few, maybe. Not many."

"I'm looking for a doctor who might have visited a patient there about thirty years ago."

"Thirty years!" The man looked as if he thought Edward was crazy. But a moment later he scratched his head. "Well, I guess it might have been old Dr. Harold. He worked here well before my time, mind you, but people still talk about him — soul of kindness and all that. I think he still sees a few patients from time to time over at his house on Lavender Lane."

Based on the man's directions, Edward had no trouble finding Dr. Harold's home. His was the largest house on a street lined with large homes. Red brick with white trim, two stories, two chimneys, and a garden in front. Clearly Dr. Harold's career had been a successful one. He couldn't have spent too much time visiting patients in Ragtown.

He won't know a thing about my mother, Edward told himself. He's probably not even the right doctor. Those thoughts pushed away his fears, made it easier to knock on the door.

The serving girl who answered looked him up and down, taking in his worn-out clothes. Edward wondered if he looked more like a beggar than a thief. "Can I help you?" she asked.

"Is the doctor at home?"

Her expression softened. "He's out just now," she said. "Would you like me to fetch the missus?"

"Thank you, but that won't be necessary. I'll come back later."

But even as he said it, Edward wondered if it was true. Would he really have the courage to try again?

"The doctor will be back soon," said the girl. "You can wait for him in the parlor if you like."

It seemed he wouldn't be forced to test his courage after all. Edward followed her into the house.

"I'll tell him you're here when he comes in," said the girl, and left him alone.

He took in his surroundings: a pretty room with a flowered carpet and lace curtains at the window. There were books on the low table in front of the love seat, one of them open. Someone, perhaps the doctor, liked to read. And someone, perhaps his wife, had left a bit of half-done embroidery beside the books — yellow flowers stitched on a white background. Edward thought of dandelions, which made him think of the princess.

But only for a moment. He closed his eyes, feeling the panic again. He could picture himself, rising up from a chair to shake the doctor's hand. He would describe his mother, and the doctor would look grave. *Yes, of course I remember the woman you describe. Her son had left her alone, and she was dying. Can you imagine? I did what I could, but . . .*

Edward heard footsteps in the hall. Was the serving girl coming back? Then he heard a voice: "Never mind, Polly. I'm sure I must have left it in the front parlor." A woman stood in the doorway. She was searching through a basket she held in her arm.

He couldn't breathe. He opened his mouth, and a choked sound came out.

The woman looked up. Her eyes were dark like his own, but her hair had gone white, and her face had grown older. The basket she was holding fell to the floor. She put her hands to her face.

"Neddy?" she said.

chapter 30

SIX WEEKS AND THREE DAYS

Adela was standing in front of the mirror in her bedroom and laughing. "I look ridiculous!" she said.

"No more so than anybody else, Your Highness," said the dress designer, who was making the last adjustments to the dandelion costume Adela was wearing. Her name was Nora, and she was a cheerful, middle-aged woman whom Adela had come to know well over the past few weeks. Nora was good at her craft. *The best in the business,* as Cecile had put it, which was why the queen had hired her to create all the royal costumes for the masquerade ball. "Don't tell Her Majesty or Lady Marguerite, but your costume is my favorite of the ones I've made," said Nora. "You're sure to have a wonderful time this evening!"

"I think I agree with you," said Adela.

She couldn't help but look forward to the ball — and the award ceremony that was to take place at it. Her father was going to bestow an honorary knighthood on both her and Garth.

"I never heard of a girl being named a knight before," Cecile had remarked.

"I'm proud of my daughter, and I want to show it." The king was not often so resolute, but when he was, Cecile knew better than to press her point.

As for the ball, Adela had asked Cecile to invite Bess and the other guests who had come to Hortensia's garden party the same day as she, Marguerite, and Garth. Adela was looking forward to seeing them again and only hoped they didn't mind wearing flower costumes. She had softened her opinion of the garden theme, thanks to Nora, who had made her see that this aspect of the evening could be entertaining. "Think of the ballroom floor as a living work of art, Your Highness," Nora had told her. "Designers from all over the kingdom will be putting forth their best effort. Trust me, it will be a sight to see." It had been fascinating to watch Nora at work, creating one costume after another. Marguerite had held true to her plan of coming as a daisy. Garth had wanted to come as himself — a gardener — but Marguerite had said no to that idea. Instead, she and Nora had secretly cooked up something *absolutely stunning*. At least that was Marguerite's description of the costume. Garth's was *absolutely ridiculous*. Adela couldn't wait to see it.

The queen had wavered between dressing as a rare purple orchid or a delicate pink rose until Nora had settled the issue for her. "I would say the rose, Your Majesty, and I can make a lovely honeybee costume for His Majesty. Very romantic, if you know what I mean." Cecile's finished gown, made of rose-colored velvet and green silk, really was a work of art, and Adela's father's costume was a marvel of construction. "Not often you get to see a king dressed up like a honeybee," Nora had remarked.

Now, in front of the full-length mirror, Adela turned slowly, admiring her own costume. Nora had made the bodice and skirt of the dress look as if they were made of large dandelion leaves. The effect was dramatic and even rather flattering. The skirt had a jagged edge that fell just above her ankles. Below the skirt, she wore stockings of light green and comfortable, dark-green satin shoes decorated with bouquets of silk dandelions.

"Very daring to show off her ankles like that," Cecile had told Nora.

"No one will mind at a masquerade ball, Your Majesty, and if I may be so bold, Her Highness does have a pretty pair of ankles."

Adela liked the way Nora spoke to Cecile—always respectful but completely confident about her work and her ideas. That was how *she* wanted to be about gardening.

The gown's neckline was formed by two long silk dandelion leaves that wrapped around Adela's arms just below her shoulders. But the crowning glory of the costume was the headdress. It consisted of a tight-fitting muslin cap with dozens of long, thin, and nearly invisible wires poking out of it. Each wire had a tuft of white feathers at the end, so that when Adela pinned up her hair and pulled on the cap, she looked as if she were wearing a cloud of dandelion seeds ready to blow away in the wind. Nora now checked to see that the cap was pinned securely in place. "Let's see it with the mask," she said.

In contrast to the rest of the costume, the mask was quite simple — leaf-green silk strengthened with muslin. Nora had spattered the silk with touches of real gold paint and then decorated it with tiny emeralds. "Stunning!" said the dressmaker as she tied the ribbons of the mask behind Adela's head.

Adela smiled at her reflection. "I've been a dandelion once before in my life, and I can assure you that this second time is much better than the first."

"Your Highness seems to have been born to play the role," said Nora. "Dandelions are my favorite flower, if you must know."

"You don't think of them as weeds?"

"Goodness, no! Dandelions mean springtime and sunshine! There's nothing that makes me as happy as seeing a field full of them. Daisies in summer give me the same feeling — oh, but that makes me think I'd better go check on Lady Marguerite's costume. She was having trouble with that collar. All those petals — I warned her that dress would be a challenge to wear."

As the dressmaker bustled out of the room, Adela sank into a chair. Nora's comment had made her think of Edward. It had been exactly six weeks and three days since he had disappeared, and she still had not completely purged him from her mind. Working in her garden helped. So did making plans for her upcoming plant-collecting expedition. Her trip had become official now; her father had said she could go in the summer. There were still details to be worked out, though. In Cecile's mind, the expedition was a garden tour, during the course of which Adela would visit the estates of wealthy families around the kingdom. She would travel by coach with a female chaperone and be treated with the appropriate royal deference wherever she visited.

Somehow, between now and the time she actually set out, Adela knew she would have to set her stepmother straight. She wouldn't be traveling by coach but would go on horseback. She wouldn't stay at Lord and Lady So-and-So's castle but would find a room at an inn. She might even camp out in the open if it suited her. She had already done as much on Flower Mountain, and she was none the worse for sleeping outdoors. As for a chaperone, Adela could see the sense in taking along a few knights in case she ran into trouble on the road. Though now that she had begun taking fencing lessons, even they might be unnecessary.

It was thanks to Cecile that Adela had taken up fencing.

At dinner one night, the queen had said, "I wonder if we shouldn't have the medal award ceremony on the day *after* the masquerade ball."

"Certainly, my dear, if you like," Adela's father had said. "Though I can't see why it matters."

"It's just that I'm afraid the award ceremony might color people's opinions of Adela. A medal for bravery and a knighthood seem so *masculine*. We don't want the guests to wonder if she'll be taking up sword fighting!"

People's opinions. Guests. By which her stepmother meant *men's opinions* and *male guests*. Adela had felt the need to make a stand. "You're so thoughtful to be concerned, Cecile. But it seems like such an inconvenience to you and the servants — not to mention the guests — to change the plans now. I insist that we keep everything as is." Then Adela had smiled broadly and added, "As for sword fighting, I think that's a marvelous idea! Just the sort of training I should have before I head off on an adventure."

"But I didn't mean—"

"May I take lessons with the fencing master, Father?"

"Certainly, my dear, if you like."

Adela's forthright attitude was an outcome of her adventure with Hortensia, and Cecile was slow to react. Before the queen could recover, everything was arranged: the medal ceremony would take place at the masquerade ball as originally planned, and Adela would take fencing lessons. These now took up the time that had once been allotted for her dancing lessons. "It's the only time the fencing master has available," Adela had told her stepmother. "But he does say that fencing will improve my overall coordination, which will in turn improve my dancing."

Whether that was true had yet to be seen. What Adela liked about fencing was that it made her feel powerful and capable. And it kept her mind busy. It was impossible to think about Edward when she was fending off an attack by one of the other students in class. It was impossible to miss him or daydream about love when she had disarmed an opponent, sending his sword flying across the room.

Adela rose from the chair and stood in front of the

mirror again, this time adopting a proper fencing pose. But at that moment, there was a knock on the door. It was Nora. "There you are!" she said. "Her Majesty has sent me to escort you down to the ballroom. You'll be announced just after the king and queen."

Adela relaxed her stance and took a final look at her costume.

If I had a garden, it would be only dandelions.

She sighed. Six weeks and three days — soon to be four, she thought.

"I'm ready," she said.

● ● ●

AT THE COMMAND OF THEIR MAJESTIES
KING ADALBERT VIII
&
QUEEN CECILE
YOUR PRESENCE IS CORDIALLY REQUESTED
AT A
MASQUERADE BALL
IN HONOR OF HER ROYAL HIGHNESS
PRINCESS ADELA

ROYAL PALACE
SATURDAY, DECEMBER 3
EIGHT O'CLOCK IN THE EVENING

Suggested Costume for Ladies:
Your Favorite Flowers

Suggested Costume for Gentlemen:
Birds, Bees & Other Garden Denizens

chapter 31

THE MASQUERADE BALL

Adela found the grand ballroom to be exactly what Nora had predicted and more. It had become a garden almost as fantastic as Hortensia's, with flowers, birds, and glittering insects swaying to the strains of the orchestra. Adela spotted a robin paired with a daylily, a hummingbird with a violet, a dragonfly with a tulip, and a fat June bug dancing with a tiny primrose who turned out to be Bess. And she nearly burst out laughing when she saw Garth leading his "daisy" onto the floor, for Nora had transformed him into a grasshopper.

Honeybee was the most popular costume for men, and Adela felt as if she had entered a hive. She danced with three honeybees in a row, a peacock, then two more bees, and then Garth, which was comical because he had no idea what to do. Nor did she, seeing as the dance was neither a waltz nor a minuet. It didn't help that the back of Garth's costume kept bumping into other couples.

"Let's sit this one out," she told him.

He looked relieved. "I'll get us some punch."

But as he moved away toward the refreshment table, Marguerite swept down on him and dragged him back to the dance floor. Adela decided she would get her own punch, and it was then that she saw the magpie.

Her heart gave a lurch. It wasn't really a magpie — only a man wearing a magpie costume. The mask did not fully cover his face; she could see he wasn't Edward. Then she looked around and realized, much to her dismay, that there were more magpies out on the ballroom floor — six or seven of them, all dressed in nearly the same costume. One was extremely tall, two were short, three were very fat. None of them was Edward.

Adela knew that Marguerite had told other people about the enchanted magpie who lived with Hortensia. *A real thief that magpie-boy turned out to be.*

Did you know that he stole a lot of jewels? Now it seemed that Marguerite's gossip had gone beyond the walls of the palace, and Adela was quite sure nothing good would have been said about Edward—nothing about his bravery or his kindness. She was grateful for her dandelion mask: otherwise she was afraid her face would betray emotions she would rather keep hidden.

"Your Highness?" said a voice behind her.

Turning around, Adela saw a young woman in a glittering red mask. Her blond head was framed by a crown of bright-red silk flowers. The skirt of her red silk ball gown was shaped like an upside-down bell-shaped flower. A poppy? thought Adela. Or maybe a tulip?

The woman lifted her mask and smiled. She was strikingly beautiful. "I beg your pardon, Your Highness. We've never met formally. But we did speak that day on Flower Mountain. I had been an amaryllis—"

"Yes! I remember! You had been enchanted for—how many years was it?"

"Twenty, Your Highness."

"Did you find your family all right?" Adela vaguely

recalled that the woman had been the daughter of someone *important*, to use one of Cecile's words. A duke or something like that.

"Yes, thank goodness!" said the woman, slipping her mask back in place. "But it was strange to come back after all this time. My sisters are all older than I am now. And my brother wasn't even born when I left home!"

"Remarkable!" said Adela, even as she thought of Edward, worried that he wouldn't find his mother after thirty years. She could only hope he had been as fortunate as this woman.

"I must tell you, Your Highness, that I adore your costume. I gather that Hortensia must have changed you into a dandelion."

"That's right."

"Did she steal your jewelry, too?"

Adela was surprised by the question. "Yes — well, not exactly . . . Why do you ask?"

The woman touched an emerald brooch that was pinned to the front of her gown. "I was wondering if your jewelry had been returned to you. I was so surprised to get mine back a few weeks ago — this brooch and all the other pieces. And earlier tonight, I met some girls — twins, you know — and they'd had theirs returned as well. Quite honestly, I never thought I'd see any of it again."

Adela looked at the brooch. "What? Are you saying that was stolen on Flower Mountain?"

"Yes, Your Highness."

"And returned?"

"By a very nice young man. Apparently he also returned some coral necklaces to those twins. And I met someone else whose pearls he'd returned."

"Who was this young man?" said Adela. "Did he give you his name?"

But a voice interrupted them.

"Adela!" Cecile was coming toward them, her hand looped through the arm of what looked like a millipede — or perhaps it was a worm.

"Adela dear, this charming caterpillar is your father's second cousin Frederick."

Adela forced a smile. "Cousin Frederick! How are you?"

"Lord Frederick would like to dance with you, Adela," said Cecile. "I've told the orchestra to play a waltz."

"Yes, but I—"

Skillfully, Cecile transferred herself from Frederick's arm to the young woman's. "What a spectacular gown you're wearing, my dear. Is it a tulip? No? An amaryllis? Oh, how lovely!"

"About that young man . . ." Adela tried to hold the attention of the woman, but the queen was already steering her in the other direction.

Frederick's voice, triumphant, boomed in Adela's ear: "I confess, Your Highness, that I have never danced with a dandelion before."

"I'm sure you haven't," said Adela. It was going to take her forever to find the amaryllis again in this crowd.

The music started up. Frederick held out his hand. But before Adela could take it, a magpie loomed behind him.

"I believe this dance is mine," said the magpie. Boldly, he stepped around Frederick, took Adela's hand, and led her into the crowd.

"Saved you from that pest, didn't I?" he said.

"Who are you?" Adela hadn't seen this particular magpie before. His costume was more elaborate than the others. He wore a feathered hood with an enormous black beak. It covered his head and face completely and made his voice sound muffled.

"A lover of dandelions, of course. They're my favorite flower."

She missed a step of the waltz, nearly falling, and the magpie pulled her toward him. "Careful there, Princess. Suppose we get out of this crowd."

He waltzed toward the edge of the crush of dancing couples. He held her hand and led her through a door and into an empty corridor. "We can dance out here, and nobody will get in our way," he told her as he drew her toward him.

"Wait!" said Adela. "Let me look at you."

He stopped, holding her in his arms, looking down at her. Through his mask, she could see that his eyes were brown. Was it possible?

"Maybe you'd like to give me a kiss," said the magpie.

She felt her face grow warm.

The magpie reached up and pulled off his hood. He leaned toward her, but Adela pulled back. The blond, ruddy-complexioned man preparing to kiss her was not Edward. "I — I'm sorry. Do I know you?"

"We met at Lady Hortensia's garden party," said the man. "I'm Anthony, Earl William's son."

Anthony . . . Earl William . . . The names sounded vaguely familiar to her. Had she seen them on Cecile's guest list?

"It was on that first day," said Anthony, clearly less than happy that Adela couldn't place him. "We barely had a chance to say hello, then everything happened, and, well, here we are now. You, as pretty a dandelion as I've ever seen, and I, an enchanted magpie. Enchanted by you, that is to say."

Adela's mouth felt dry. She did remember Anthony now—barely. Certainly not well enough to want to kiss him! Gently, she tried to push him away.

His arms encircled her again, and she gave a more forceful push. "I'm sorry, but I—I don't really feel like dancing."

What she felt like was crying. Once again, she was grateful for her mask.

"I could take you back inside and get you some punch," Anthony said hopefully.

"No, thank you. I think I need some air."

"I'll take you outside," he offered.

No!" Adela had to force politeness into her voice. "I prefer to be alone, thank you."

When he was gone, she felt the threat of tears again. I cannot — I will not cry, thought Adela.

A set of glass doors at the far end of the corridor led to a terrace that overlooked the palace gardens. She headed toward the doors, pushed them open, and stepped out into the cold December night. She took several slow breaths to calm herself, watching the air turn white in front of her. And then, as she had done again and again for the past six weeks and three days, she forced herself to think of something other than Edward.

She thought of her garden. It lay out there in the darkness, asleep under a layer of snow, waiting for spring when the bulbs she had planted would come up. Garth was going to help her get the garden ready for summer, and he would take care of it while she was away on her plant-hunting expedition.

Behind her, she could hear music and laughter. It was hard to believe that she had been part of that only moments ago. She would have to go back inside and pretend that she was still having a good time. She hoped she could carry it off. Maybe she could — if only she could stop thinking about Edward. Not that she was having much success with that.

At least she now knew he was alive. He must have been the one who had returned the jewels to the amaryllis and the coral bells. But why had he taken the jewels in the first place, without telling her he was going away? If he had felt about her the way she felt about him — if he had loved her — he never would have done that.

This must be what people mean by having a broken heart, thought Adela.

Then she remembered Hortensia, whose heart really *had* been broken.

Because she kept it in a box. At least I'm not like *her*, Adela told herself. I don't suppose Hortensia ever really loved anybody. Not that love is doing me any good right now.

She must make herself think about other things.

Tonight her father would award her the King Ival Medal and a knighthood. That was a good thing. Adela looked out at the garden and thought about the spring, when her flowers would come up. That was a good thing as well. And the summer, when she would go on her journey. She would travel the world and learn all that she could so that someday she could create gardens that would make people look and look again.

"I'll be all right," said Adela.

Someday, she thought.

chapter 32

TELLING EVERYTHING

He would tell her everything . . . if he could only find her.

Edward stood in the middle of the floor, surrounded by dancing flowers and birds and insects. Where was the princess?

He had spotted her almost as soon as he had come into the ballroom. It wasn't hard to miss the dandelion in the crowd of more showy blooms. But a footman had stopped him near the door.

"At the queen's request, would the good sir be so kind as to wear this mask?"

"A mask?"

"Her Majesty was aware that some guests might come unprepared. . . ."

He hadn't known about the costumes. *A ball in honor of the princess* was all he had heard, which had been enough to bring him here tonight to find her. But he *was* coming uninvited, so the mask could be helpful. He had stopped to put it on, watching as the princess talked to some people — a lady dressed up to look like a red flower, a lady dressed up like a rose, and a man dressed up like a worm. Edward had pushed his way toward them, but before he could reach the princess, the worm had led her out among the dancing couples. And then — of all things — a magpie had swooped in and snatched her from the worm, dancing away with her and disappearing into the crowd.

Now she was gone.

Edward had circled the floor several times already, looking for her. He was about to try again when he saw someone he knew. Or, rather, two people he knew — the twin sisters from Hortensia's garden. Despite their masks, he could tell who they were because they were wearing the coral beads he had returned to them last week. It had been the sisters who had told him about the ball. "We can wear our beads to the royal ball next week. It's being given in honor of the princess, and we're going to dress up as coral bells." He hadn't known then what they'd meant about "dressing up as coral bells." Now he understood, for the sisters were wearing gowns that looked rather like leaves and hats covered with tiny pink blossoms. And over there was a daisy wearing diamond earrings. Edward could guess who *she* was. *Marguerite*, he remembered. She was dancing with a grasshopper who looked familiar. *The gardener.*

It was only then that it occurred to him that the entire ballroom was meant to be a garden. Not just any garden, he thought. *Hers.* What else could explain the magpie he had seen? He looked around, noticing for the first time that there were other magpies in the room. His eyes came to rest on one halfway across the floor, talking to a daffodil. Was it the same one he had seen before?

Edward walked toward him. "Excuse me, sir."

"Yes?"

"I was looking for the princess. . . ."

The magpie chuckled. "Good luck, there!" He nodded toward the back of the ballroom. "She's out in the hallway — said she wanted to be alone."

There was a door at the back of the room. He slipped through it and found himself in a hallway as grand as the ballroom, with chandeliers down the length of it, a thick red carpet, and gilded furniture to sit on. But there was no sign of the princess.

It was his mother who had insisted he come to the palace. She had guessed how he felt about the princess. "Of course you must return the jewels to their owners, Neddy. But after that, you must go see her. You ran off without telling her where you were going or what you were doing." He had made up his mind that his mother was right. He needed to talk to the princess. He needed to explain his actions and apologize for his cowardice. But first he needed to find her.

He shivered. It was cold in the hallway, and he noticed a pair of glass doors in the distance. The left-hand one was ajar, letting in the night air. He walked toward it.

And saw her. She was standing outside, her dandelion crown lit up by the moon, her breath making a mist in the air. She must be freezing, thought Edward.

He pushed the door open. "Princess?"

As she turned, the feathers of her crown gleamed

like diamonds in the moonlight. She looked even more beautiful than he remembered. "Edward?" she said.

She came inside, and he closed the door.

"Is it really you?" she said.

He pulled off his mask.

"Where have you been?" she asked. "When you left, I thought —"

"That I was a thief," he finished for her.

"No! I thought you might have been hurt — or killed . . . something awful."

Which was what his mother had said she would think. *The princess won't know what's happened to you, Neddy. She'll worry. . . .*

"I'm sorry," he said. "I went to look for my mother, and —"

"Did you find her? Is she all right?"

He had expected doubt or even anger from the princess. But he heard only sympathy and concern in her voice.

"Yes," he said. "Well, I mean, she's older now. But she's happy and healthy. She married a doctor after I left. And she had more children. I have a half-brother and half-sister who are older than me. . . ."

"She must have been so happy to see you!"

His mother had cried. He'd had to hold on to her to keep her from falling down. "She was happy," said Edward.

But the princess's interest in his mother — her interest in *him* — was distracting him from his purpose.

You must tell her how you feel, Neddy. You must tell her everything. . . .

"Please," he said, "could we talk for a bit? I know you want to be alone, but —"

"Alone? I don't want to be alone!"

She sat down on a small couch. Edward sat beside her. He began with the speech he had rehearsed in his mind. "I need to tell you how I came to be at Hortensia's and why she did what she did to me."

"I know why. She was a witch who liked to hurt people."

How easy it would be to let it go at that. To place all of the blame on Hortensia. To avoid having the princess think the worst of him.

But he hadn't come here to do what was easy. He had come here to do what was right, and so he went on. "When I was little, there was only my mother to take care of me. My father died before I was born, and we never had much money. We were always hungry, and as soon as I was old enough, I got a job helping a man clean chimneys. I didn't like the work. It was hot and dirty, but I noticed something. I saw that the people whose chimneys we cleaned weren't like my mother and me. They had nice things. They had plenty to eat. They even had fires to keep them warm in winter, which was why they needed a skinny little boy like me to sweep out their chimneys."

The princess must have heard the bitterness in his voice. "That made you angry."

"It was unfair. Why should other people have so much, and we so little? So one day, after I'd swept the chimneys at a big, fancy house, I noticed a bit of money sitting on the mantel. It was only a few coins, and it seemed to me nobody would ever miss them, and I slipped them into my pocket. But my master saw me and made me put the money back. And when we were outside again, he kicked me onto the pavement and told me to be on my way; he couldn't have a thief working for him."

"You were only a boy," said the princess.

"I was. But that still doesn't forgive what I did next. I should have told my mother what had happened.

I should have at least tried to find another job. But I was ashamed of having been caught, and I was still angry about how unfair it was — other people having so much. So instead I took to stealing. It was only food at first, and I told myself we deserved that food, just like the coins I'd tried to take. But after a while, I got to stealing more than food — things I could sell for money.

"It wasn't long before my mother found out. She made me promise I'd never steal again. So I promised and said I'd find work. But I went right on stealing and told her the money came from odd jobs I'd picked up. Time and time again, I lied to her. She'd gotten sick, and we had nothing to eat and barely a room to live in — I didn't know what else to do. Besides, no one would have hired me. I was too well known as a thief. That's what I told myself, anyway. I confess I never actually tried to find work."

He felt sick with the shame of it and wondered what the princess thought of him. But she was only listening, waiting for him to go on.

"Then one day," he continued, "we found a letter pushed under our door. It was pink, and it smelled like perfume."

The princess's eyes grew wide. "Hortensia!"

He nodded. "I didn't know why it had come. Why should I be invited to a party that must surely be for rich people? My mother asked the same question — said it must be a mistake and I'd better not go. So I told her another lie. I told her I knew Lady Hortensia. I made up some nonsense about pulling her out of the way of a runaway horse and how she was grateful to me. I told my mother the invitation meant good things and that Lady Hortensia would help us out of our troubles. I doubt my mother believed me, but she was so sick by then, she didn't have the strength to argue. I told myself I would go to the party, and I would steal a few things from the wealthy people there. Then I would come back, and I would find a doctor and pay all the rent we owed, and it would be the last time I ever stole anything.

"Or lied," he added softly.

"Anyway, when I got to the party, I sneaked into the house while everyone was admiring the garden, and I found all her jewels. But Hortensia caught me stealing and — well, you know what she did. And now you know why. Because I'm a thief."

"You *were* a thief," said the princess. "You're not

anymore. I spoke to someone tonight who told me you had returned her jewels. Did you return everything?"

"All that I could. But there were some things I didn't recognize. I suppose she must have stolen those before I came to her garden party." Edward reached into his coat and pulled out a small bundle. "These are for you. Maybe you and your father can return them, the way you said."

"Why didn't you tell me any of this before? I could have helped you."

"I—I didn't want to be there when you realized what I was," said Edward. "When you realized I was a thief."

"Oh, Edward! Just because you were once a thief doesn't mean you are now. Obviously, you're not! Why, even when you disappeared with the jewels, I never thought for a moment that you'd stolen them."

These were the words he had dreamed of hearing her say! But Edward could still hear another voice in his mind. "That's not what Hortensia said. She said I would be a thief forever."

"Hortensia said all kinds of horrible, untrue things," said the princess.

There was something in her voice that made him

remember that last night, when Hortensia had made her cry. What cruel, untrue things had she said to the princess before turning her into a dandelion?

"She was full of lies," said Edward.

"Yes, she was."

He took her hand. "If you hadn't come to her garden party — if I hadn't met you — I would still be there. You saved me."

"If it hadn't been for you, I would be a dead dandelion," said the princess. "We saved each other, you and I." She squeezed his hand.

I've done it, thought Edward. I've told her everything, and it's all right.

Or, rather, *almost* everything.

"Adela?"

She smiled, the color deepening in her cheeks. He had never seen anything so beautiful.

"I love you," he said.

She held his gaze. "I love you, too."

chapter 33
SUMMER

One morning, late in June, everyone was up by dawn. The king and queen, Henry, Marguerite, and Garth came down to the palace courtyard to say good-bye to Adela and Edward.

Cecile was fussing. "I can't believe you're not taking a carriage. And you're wearing trousers, Adela! Promise me you'll wear something more suitable when you visit Lady Isabel's garden. "

Adela was checking the girth on her saddle. "I promise to clean up for Lady Isabel, Cecile. And it's much easier for us to go by horseback. Besides, we'll need a wagon eventually, but not until we get back from our voyage. We may need two or three, depending on how many plants we collect. I'll have to hire them once we know."

"It all seems so reckless!" said Cecile. "Sailing off to the ends of the earth —"

"We are not sailing to the ends of the earth. I've shown you the map."

"You and Edward might at least think about getting married first —"

"Getting married can wait, Cecile. Collecting plants in the right season cannot. And if you're still worried about a chaperone, rest assured that Dr. Sophus will be with us for the entire journey. Besides, you haven't got time to plan a wedding for us. You'll be too busy getting ready for Garth and Marguerite's in September."

"You *will* be back for it?" said Marguerite, repeating a concern she had expressed many times already.

"We wouldn't miss it for the world!"

"I do wish you would take along a few of your father's knights," said the queen.

"Edward and I *are* knights, Cecile! Besides, in three days, we'll be aboard one of the royal ships. We'll be fine until then. We're going to stay at an inn tonight, and tomorrow we'll be at Edward's mother's house," said Adela. And after that, who knows? she thought.

They might camp out under the stars. No sense mentioning *that* to Cecile.

"But the islands sound so . . . dangerous!" said the queen — not for the first time.

"Now, then, dear," said the king, "I'm sure Edward and Sophus will take good care of Adela."

"More likely she'll take care of us," said Edward, who was coming across the courtyard with Adela's tutor. They were leading three horses — two of them saddled and ready to ride, the other laden down with bundles. "Adela's better with her sword than anyone I can think of, not to mention the fact that she's won a medal for bravery."

"Father gave *you* the same medal, *Sir* Edward," said Adela. "Don't forget that."

"Well, then, I guess I can probably manage to crack someone over the head with a shovel if I need to."

"Speaking of gardening equipment, have we got it all?"

"Everything on your list."

"And I have the maps," said Dr. Sophus.

Adela was thrilled that her tutor was coming with them. In addition to bringing maps, she knew he had packed a collection of books about the local flora of the islands they would be visiting, an almanac for predicting weather conditions, and some poetry. "To entertain us in the evenings," he had explained.

Adela hugged her father and Garth and exchanged kisses with Marguerite and Cecile. She tried to give Henry a kiss, but her brother refused to look at her, burying his face in Cecile's dress. He was angry that she was leaving.

"We'll be back soon, Henry. We'll bring you all kinds of surprises!" she told him.

"Flowers and bushes and trees—we'll bring you your very own jungle," said Edward.

Henry peeked out at them, his attention caught by the word *jungle*. A moment later, he threw his arms around Edward and then Adela.

"Good-bye!"

And then they were off. The palace and the royal city fell away behind them, and it occurred to Adela that the last time she had traveled along this road, she had been going to Hortensia's garden party. Trapped in a carriage, tied up in a corset, her feet pinched by her shoes, with no idea whatsoever that she was about to meet up with a witch—or an enchanted magpie!

How much better to be riding in the open air, wearing comfortable trousers and boots. Not to mention having Edward as company. She smiled at him, only to see that he looked pensive.

"What is it?" she said.

"I was thinking about Hortensia—about witches, really. Do you suppose there are any more of them?"

"Maybe," said Adela. "I haven't given it much thought, really."

Dr. Sophus, riding just behind them, chimed in, "Right you are to keep it in mind, I think, Sir Edward. I wouldn't be surprised to see all those witches and wizards who were chased away by Hortensia come out of hiding now that she's gone."

"Do you really think there could be a resurgence of magic in the kingdom?" said Adela. She felt obliged to hide the excitement she felt about this possibility.

"Best to keep an open mind, I always say," said Dr. Sophus. "Best to be alert. Who knows? We may even see a return of dragons. Just in case, I've brought along some books that may come in handy—practical aspects of magic, the habits of dragons, and so on."

"I'm glad you didn't mention any of this in front of Cecile. She never would have let us leave!"

"That thought had occurred to me, Your Highness," said Dr. Sophus.

Edward let out a laugh, then tried to look more serious. "What if we meet up with a dragon?" he said. "I mean, I know we can handle ourselves admirably if we encounter a witch, but . . ."

"A dragon could be a problem," finished Adela. "On the other hand, I have my sword. And you have a shovel. And Dr. Sophus has his books. I expect we'll do just fine."

KRISTIN KLADSTRUP is the author of the middle-grade novel *The Book of Story Beginnings* and the picture book *The Gingerbread Pirates*, illustrated by Matt Tavares. About *Garden Princess*, she says, "I love gardens and books about princesses, so it doesn't surprise me that the story combines these two favorite things. What does surprise me is the magpie. I didn't expect him to show up!" Kristin Kladstrup lives with her family near Boston.